The
SHAMAN *and the*
STRANGER

The
SHAMAN *and the*
STRANGER

DENNIS MCKAY

iUniverse®

THE SHAMAN AND THE STRANGER

This is a work of fiction. All of the characters, names, incidents, organizations, and dialogue in this novel are either the products of the author's imagination or are used fictitiously.

iUniverse books may be ordered through booksellers or by contacting:

iUniverse
1663 Liberty Drive
Bloomington, IN 47403
www.iuniverse.com
1-800-Authors (1-800-288-4677)

Because of the dynamic nature of the Internet, any web addresses or links contained in this book may have changed since publication and may no longer be valid. The views expressed in this work are solely those of the author and do not necessarily reflect the views of the publisher, and the publisher hereby disclaims any responsibility for them.

Any people depicted in stock imagery provided by Thinkstock are models, and such images are being used for illustrative purposes only. Certain stock imagery © Thinkstock.

ISBN: 978-1-4917-6178-6 (sc)
ISBN: 978-1-4917-6177-9 (e)

Library of Congress Control Number: 2015903890

Print information available on the last page.

iUniverse rev. date: 03/26/2015

CHAPTER 1

Portland, Oregon
1999

From behind a wall of shrubbery, the old man emerged. Leaning on his cane, he rotated himself in two stilted movements before making his way into the park—one step forward, lead with the cane, bad leg out to the side.

At his bench, he removed from a pocket of his tweed jacket a sandwich baggie, and from the other pocket he took a paperback. There was a weariness about this relic of a man as he sat slumped-shouldered with book in hand, slowly eating and reading, with an air of isolation hanging about his manner as though he were the lone survivor of some long-ago horror.

When he finished, he placed the book down at his side, brushed each hand with the back of the other, and then paused for a long, careful moment. He then removed a cigarette case from an inside pocket, secured a cigarette in the corner of his mouth, and then from the same pocket took a flint lighter, striking the spark wheel three times before a flame emerged. His mannerisms seemed foreign as he slowly inhaled and exhaled the cigarette secured between his middle and ring finger—what a gift to enjoy.

At first, Peter Richards had paid him little attention, but as time went by, and every day the old man arrived in the park at eleven thirty, Peter began to look for him from his office window. He had considered going down to introduce himself. But the man would know he was being watched, ruining something better left alone.

Grudgingly, Peter turned his attention from the window to his desk. "Yeah, yeah." He heard the "woe is me" tone in his voice but had not a clue what to do about it. *It* had snuck up on him much like moisture on an exposed iron pipe, gradually corroding the surface until the reddish, scaly oxide began eating into the interior. Nothing in this life seemed clear-cut, everything redundant—"been there, done that."

He raised the desk's adjustable surface to a tilted position. At his workshop at home, he had assembled the main frame with mortise and tenon, and dowel rods for the retractable work surface, not a single nail used.

From his drawer, he removed a numbered list of modifications to an upscale office building. Peter had never liked his creations tampered with. Walking a fine line between acceding to a client's wishes and maintaining his sense of architectural integrity had been a strong suit. A meeting would take place where Peter would explain in layman's terms how he envisioned the final product. He never raised his voice, never pushed too hard, and usually received concessions he could live with.

Scrolling down the list, his finger stopped at number 4: "Need to cut $25,000.00 from atrium budget, but keep the marble floor and fountain." He leaned back in his chair, stretched his arms overhead with fingers interlaced, and muttered to the ceiling, "You have got to be kidding me."

Through the glass wall of his office, Peter saw Dory stationed at her desk sifting through mail. Beyond Dory was "the compound," as Peter had affectionately designated the open space, where young interns and draftsmen stood at their drafting desks, all seemingly immersed in the world of architectural design. He had named the space as sort of a joke, but when he looked *compound* up in the dictionary, he discovered a definition that truly fit: "to produce or create by combining two or more parts, aspects, etc." He then looked up *aspect*: "a way in which something can be viewed by the mind." That was what had inspired Peter, creating in his mind a functioning and aesthetically pleasing structure where there had been nothing before or something dilapidated and used up. It was a feeling that Peter used to cherish, but now it seemed to have deserted him, and it left in its place a general disinterest in not only architecture but every aspect of his life. And time, which in the past he never seemed to have enough of, had conspired against him as though this day may never end. Only one thing to do.

"Dory, I have a meeting in Belmont and another in the Hawthorne district."

Forty, heavyset, career secretary, Dory looked up from her computer screen. "Meetings?"

"That's right, Dory, meetings."

She leafed through the appointment book. "I don't—"

"See you tomorrow."

Peter stopped short of the entrance to his community—anything to break the routine. Parked along the side of the road, he noted chinked mortar in the first *H* of "Hemlock Hills" on one of the two brick columns, the one to his left. The brickwork was for decorative purposes only, a welcoming construct of eight-foot-high walls of alternating stretching and heading courses of red colonial brick, extending twenty feet on each side. Prior to the wall's construction, Peter had gotten hold of a copy of the blueprints and took issue with the utilitarian twin-walled design. He offered to design gratis a protruding and recessed, two-way arched brick entrance with stone pilasters, but the developer wouldn't go for it. Rectangles and straight lines were never Peter's cup of tea; he preferred arches and irregularity in form. But, since English ivy covered both columns and walls, it all now seemed rather moot. And though some members of the community considered the small-leafed plant invasive, Peter had grown to admire its dark-green beauty and ability to survive.

A few summers back at a community meeting, one resident, an older woman, had blared her displeasure. "It is a pernicious scourge," she had said in a raspy voice that reminded Peter of an ornery nanny goat. "English ivy," she said as she rapped her cane on the floor, "needs to be banned from the neighborhood. And the quicker the better."

But the members of the landscape committee politely demurred. Undeterred, each summer she would make her feelings known about that insidious weed, English ivy. As a member of the committee, Peter felt conflicted. Having seen firsthand the damage ivy did to trees and structures, he felt obligated to come to her defense, but the other, stronger part, strangely fascinated by its resilient beauty, remained silent.

Shifting into drive, he accelerated into his community. It was hard to believe it had been fourteen years. After Devon was born, Peter and Debra had put their condo on the market and began looking for a home. The search ended when they found Hemlock Hills under construction. The detailed craftsmanship of the neo-craftsman bungalows and ranch-style homes impressed Peter and Debra, as did the cul-de-sacs and winding streets lined by newly planted trees, locust and maple prominent, and nary a hemlock to be found—all cut down at groundbreaking. The houses now had that lived-in homey look, and along with the now middling-sized trees lining the streets, the neighborhood had attained understated character that only time allowed.

When they first moved in, Peter and Deb thought it would be only a couple of years before they would move on, purchasing a vacant property or a teardown. Peter would design a grand home with a basement, no less, which was not standard in Portland. But their house seemed to fit them. There were only the three of them, so why live in more space than needed?

Through the windshield, shafts of glistening sunlight splayed through the green foliage, which soon would transform into a rainbow of colors before fading away to a wrinkled, dying brown. The rapid tweet of a swallow, which Peter imagined flapping and gliding from tree to tree, cut through the purring of the car's engine as though singing directly to him. How lonely it sounded, a soul mate.

He parked in front of the detached garage, which he used as a workshop. A loose shingle hanging precariously over the edge of the breezeway caught Peter's eye. He ignored the little voice that told him to press the garage door opener; get out a hammer, a couple of roofing nails, and the ladder; and nail it back up. It didn't seem worth the bother. Nothing seemed worth the bother. To say he wasn't himself would be an understatement.

His gaze drifted over to the window box under the bay window of the family room, teeming with snapdragons. More out of habit, he took a cursory inventory of the yard, the laurel and azalea bushes along the picket fence and the lilac in the front, its mulch bed circled in a stone border. Peter's neglect was evident, for the beds needed weeding, the yard mowing, and the bushes trimming.

He trudged up the flagstone walk, which he had mortared over the existing concrete the first year they moved in. After completing the masonry job on the walk and front stoop, he had snipped shoots of English ivy from the brick wall at the entrance to Hemlock Hills, transplanting it along his front walk. He bordered it from the lawn with old bricks that he salvaged from a job site. Within a couple of years, he had a thicket that needed constant trimming. The old lady with the cane had been right—ivy was a cunning, ruthless plant when left unchecked. Like everything of late, he had not tended to his ivy, allowing it to spread onto the lawn and walk.

In the past, Peter would sometimes take a moment before entering his home, envisioning it on blueprints, drifting from room to room like imaginary smoke. He floated into the foyer. His home office was on one side to the left, and the den was on the right; up the steps there was a spacious landing with a built-in bookcase and beadboard trim. The master bedroom overlooked the yard, the guest bedroom the driveway, and nestled in the rear was Deb's sewing room. Back downstairs, the foyer flowed down two steps to the kitchen—redesigned by Peter with Deb's input—which, after fourteen years, had maintained a quality appearance with granite countertops, stainless-steel appliances, and glass-and-wood cabinets. Off the kitchen nook down a hallway were Devon's bedroom and the laundry room.

But now, even the pleasure of envisioning the interior of his home drew no interest. No longer did it seem something to be admired, but only a box to exist in.

He opened the door as though not to wake anyone. In the kitchen, Debra was preparing dinner unaware of his arrival. She was a slender woman with a lovely face highlighted by a pinch of pink high in the cheeks, chestnut-colored hair that fell to her shoulders, and wide-set brown eyes, beautiful eyes that seemed to transmit a certain hospitable warmth. Even at forty-three there remained that girl-next-door look about her.

He stepped into the foyer onto a slate floor that he had installed their first year in the house. It had been a fun project, with Debra helping with the pattern design. Actually, they'd had a disagreement beforehand. Debra had wanted a repeating pattern, Peter random. They settled on half the pattern repeated, the other half random.

Debra had helped with mixing mortar and cleaning up loose grout around the joints while Peter cut and placed the stones. Both had been pleased with the finished product.

Entering the foyer had given Peter a sense of home from not only the slate floor but also the dark-blue lattice wallpaper that Debra had hung. Now the foyer seemed cold and unwelcoming. It didn't feel like home.

He didn't feel like himself anymore—rather a stranger in his own body, a stranger in his own home.

The aroma of beef stew drew his attention back to the kitchen, where Debra sprinkled seasoning into a pot. But this was not the same Debra. A glint of uncertainty hovered around the eyes, dampening the warm glow; the shoulders hunched as she moved in a regimented manner like a marionette being pulled by unsure hands, all collateral damage from Peter's malaise.

He closed the door to announce his presence. Debra wiped her hands on her apron and forced a hesitant smile. "You're early, Peter."

A nervous, unsure tremor in her voice seemed to ring in Peter's brain like an alarm going off. "Early, late—what's the difference?" he said as he entered the kitchen.

Debra looked at her husband, her squinting gaze speaking volumes, so different from the soft smile and shining eyes. Neither had ever been a big talker, but there had always been a tacit understanding of comfortable love, like a pair of old shoes that belonged together, without a lot of hoopla in each other's presence.

For years Peter had looked forward to coming home to Deb. He hadn't even had to be in the same room, as long as he was under the same roof near her calm, steady presence.

Peter poured a glass of water from the tap, took a sip, and stared vacantly out the kitchen window. Debra glanced at her husband with a look that said, Why are you drinking tap water when there's a five-gallon jug of purified water that you insisted on the family using?

He ignored the stare, wishing he were alone, wishing he were anywhere other than under his wife's watchful eye.

"Peter, we need to talk." Her tone crackled with a palpable, kinetic friction. And, Peter realized, so did his.

Before all this, there had been a gentleness in their exchanges that was short and sweet—so very sweet. Their world of equilibrium had been upended by one of constant tension.

"What?" Peter heard the impatience in his voice.

Debra started to speak but then seemed to think better of it as she removed a canister from the cabinet. She turned and faced her husband, looking both impatient and fearful. "I'm not talking about you, Peter, but our son." She sprinkled a tablespoon of brown sugar into the pot and said, "Why aren't you two spending time out back anymore?"

Peter leaned on the counter, focusing on a ten-foot-high platform in the middle of the backyard that he had designed and built for Devon's eighth birthday to teach his son the rudiments of stargazing. "Beats me."

Debra slammed the cabinet door shut, startling herself, not only by the severity of the act but also by the fact that she had been the cause. His apathy was rocking her world. "That's not good enough." She took a wooden spoon leaning on a stone trivet and stirred the pot of stew. Then she stopped.

"Peter, please snap out of whatever it is you're in and come back to me." In three stiff gestures Debra dispersed another tablespoon of brown sugar into the stew. "Also, the history teacher called—he's failed two quizzes, and a report is overdue."

Peter continued to look out the window ... past the platform, the hammock under the red oak tree rocked gently in a breeze. "Is he home?"

"Devon is sinking into a very sad and unhappy state, Peter."

"You did not answer my question. Is. He. Home?"

Debra raised the back of her hand to her brow and gave her head a little shake. "Yes, he is, and you need to talk with him."

"All right," he said as he looked toward the hallway leading to his son's room. "I'll talk to him."

Peter tapped on Devon's door and opened it. "Dev."

From his desk, Devon looked up at his father and then returned his attention to an open textbook as though trying to look busy. The boy was more lank and bone than either parent, but he did have Peter's hair, which Debra said reminded her of dark wheat rippling in a breeze, and his mother's soft brown eyes. It seemed he would grow into a tall, long-limbed young man, opposite of Peter's sturdy physique, which years of distance running had honed to a lean muscularity.

Just last year in eighth grade Devon had been a popular boy, but after his first month of high school he had become a lonely child. He needed a father to put an arm on his shoulder to let him know that it would be all right.

In his haze, Peter could see the problem and formulate the words, but he could not get them out of his mouth. This son whom he loved like no one else, this boy, with whom he had always had a marvelous relationship, was floundering.

Peter approached Devon. "What's with the phone call from the history teacher?"

"Mom make you come in here?" There was annoyance in his voice.

"Don't talk to me like that," Peter warned. "No arguments. Your mother and I expect better. Got it?"

A smug smile formed in the corner of the boy's mouth. "Yeah, I got it."

Peter leaned over Devon, closed an astronomy book, and tapped a history book. "Let's start spending time with this."

"For your information, I have a science exam tomorrow on the constellations."

Peter pounded his fist on the desk, rattling a lamp and causing Devon to jump in his seat.

The room was suddenly brittle with silence.

Peter cleared his throat as if to start anew and said in a voice as gentle as he could muster, "An exam on the constellations?" A shudder of regret passed through Peter. How wonderful those nights on the platform under a dark, starry sky had been, sharing a common bond with his only child. "Look, Devon, you could have passed that test when you were in fourth grade."

Devon looked at his father, and in his eyes, for the first time, Peter saw contempt.

CHAPTER 2

"We're designing a retreat, not a fortress." Peter was in the compound, jabbing his finger on a blueprint. "It needs fluted pilasters and balustrades."

The young architect looked up from his drawing table and offered a wary look at his boss. In the past they had enjoyed exchanging ideas over design, both using humor to make their point, but no more. "Yes, I understand."

Peter nodded okay and headed over to Dory's desk, where she was opening mail. He started to speak when a sudden, throbbing pain pounded his skull. He rubbed his temple with his thumb and forefinger.

"Peter, you okay?"

"Aspirin?"

Dory removed a vial of Tylenol from her drawer.

"No," he growled. "I said aspirin."

Dory's round, florid face pinched with hurt. She was a big admirer of her boss, but lately she had been getting her feelings hurt on a regular basis. "No aspirin, Peter."

Peter rummaged through his desk, finding what he was looking for. He chewed down three tablets as the hammering throb pulverized his skull. Never in his life had he experienced the likes of this. Was this a migraine? He leaned forward in his chair, put his head in his hands, and remained as still as possible.

After fifteen minutes the pain subsided, but it left him shaky. At a compartmentalized shelf crammed with architectural manuals, Peter removed one on window design, opened it to the section on estimated design pressure, found what he was looking for, and returned the book to the shelf. Normally, he would have taken a moment to look down memory lane at pictures hanging on the wall. One was of Peter crossing the finish line at a 20K a few years back when he finished third in his first year in the over-forty age group, another of Debra sitting on a rock overlooking a river on their first canoe trip together in college, and in the middle was a photo of seven-year-old Devon washing up at a creek on his first campout. But like many things of late, he ignored the photos and returned to his desk.

He removed from his drawer a rough spec sheet for a six-thousand-square-foot arts-and-crafts bungalow on a lake. Peter looked for aesthetic discrepancies in a rough draft before okaying it on to the next of the many phases prior to submission of the final proposal.

First, did he find the design pleasing? Yes, the front façade had wood plank shutters, a stone finish at the base, wood columns on stone pillars ... He paused as he felt a cloud of light-headedness.

The rear of the house had an abundance of outdoor views with bay windows at the screened porch, the great room on the main floor, the master sitting area ... Peter's power of concentration, an ally in his career, had slowly been eroding away the last few months, but he had experienced nothing like this. Was he coming down with something? He rarely got sick.

Dory came in and placed the mail she had sorted through into his incoming tray. "Here you go, Peter," she said.

Normally when he didn't want her to leave right away, he would strike up a lighthearted conversation outside the purview of work for a minute or two. But his silence was a signal that she had come to expect of late.

"Want it closed?" Dory asked with her hand on the doorknob, already knowing the answer.

"Yes."

Dory stayed at the door for a moment and glanced at her boss from the corner of her eye.

"What is it, Dory?"

"Bill called. He and Tim are coming down in ten minutes."

"Bill and Tim? What are you talking about?"

Dory raised her hands to indicate that was all she knew.

Peter uttered a grunt that caused Dory to wince before he motioned for her to close the door.

Tim Heiden, Bill Ebert, and Peter had been friends in architectural school at the University of Oregon. After graduation, they had gone their separate ways but with the goal of someday starting up a firm as equal partners.

A few years later, Tim's father had loaned them seed money to form Ebert, Heiden & Richards Architects. At first, their only employee had been a secretary. But they grew the business and saved enough to eventually make a down payment to build their own office building, with additional rental space that could later be used for future expansion.

Peter had found a half-acre lot of an abandoned family restaurant that had gone out of business after fifty years. It was a great location with the winding Wycee Creek as a divider from woodlands owned by the county. But the restaurant had grandfathered commercial zoning, and there was no guarantee the property would maintain that status.

The three partners realized the building's design and its impact on the ecology were critical. They lived in Oregon, after all. Peter wanted a brick exterior with casement windows; Tim, glass and steel; and Bill was fine either way but stressed the importance of energy efficiency. Finally, they settled on a three-story brick-and-glass structure with large low-emissivity windows that dominated the façade. The building had solar panels on the south side of the eco-friendly polymer paneled roof, with four wind turbines to harness the northwest wind.

They had gotten a tacit okay from officials at the Planning and Zoning Commission, with whom Peter had built relationships over the years, but they had to get the approval of the civic association.

Peter went door-to-door with blueprints in hand, emphasizing the ecological aspects of the building. He then organized a civic meeting at the local middle school.

The standing-room only audience in the gym-auditorium was a collection ranging from men in business suits to folks in jeans and plaid shirts. Standing onstage behind a lectern, Peter gave a brief introduction and then said, "Green architecture is a form of environmentally sensitive design and construction." He stopped to lower the volume on the microphone and also to give the audience time to settle down. "Energy-saving, sustainable development, and natural materials are all hallmarks of this type of construction, and we believe in it. We are also sensitive to the impact of the construction on the environment after the job is complete."

He paused for a moment, as late arrivers were taking seats and drawing attention. Others were talking among themselves. "Has anyone heard of daylighting?" Peter had asked the audience. Without waiting for a response, he continued, "It's the use of natural light to illuminate the building, reducing the need for electricity." People were now seated and the talking had died down, but an air of doubt hung in the room—prove it.

A woman in the front row wearing overalls and a blue-checkered shirt had a lived-in face of an old hippie, wrinkled and weathered, that had found true solace in Mother Earth. There was something instinctual in her gaze, a trust in Peter Richards as though he were capable of doing great good.

Peter gathered momentum from her bright, alert eyes as if harnessing her energy.

"Daylighting is the result of a combination of art and science, of architecture and engineering ..." After a few minutes, he had their undivided attention.

A man in a gray flannel suit raised a hand while Peter was in the middle of his PowerPoint presentation on daylighting. Peter asked him to stand. He identified himself as a civil engineer and had a skeptical expression that only an engineer could muster. It was a look of a no-nonsense individual, a man of numbers and cold, hard facts ... a man like many Peter had met in his years in business. The man had read some literature claiming that daylighting let in too much heat and was not efficient.

"That is an urban legend that has become myth," Peter said in a tone ringing with authority. "I have the art and science of architecture on my side. I, for one, do not believe in myth."

A murmur of respectful interest had come over the audience, save for the old hippie woman, who had a wise, quizzical look that said, Young man, there are still things for you to learn in this life.

Peter said to the engineer, "Properly designed daylighting screens out 99 percent of the sun's heat while providing fifty foot-candles of light." He placed his fingertips on his chest and said, "Let me reiterate. I have the art and science of architecture on my side." He opened his hands toward the engineer in a conciliatory manner. "I am certain that being an engineer, a civil engineer, you would agree with that."

The engineer peppered Peter on various building codes. Peter went over each code and explained how they planned to meet it. Finally, the engineer sat down with an expression of grudging satisfaction.

Peter then handed out a pamphlet he had written and designed describing energy-saving methods around the home.

Two days later, Ebert, Heiden & Richards received approval of commercial zoning. That was Peter Richards at his peak—envision, problem solve, and design.

It had been a major win for the nascent partnership, which now had over sixty employees, with teams of architects and draftsmen occupying all three floors of their building. There were no more renters.

The three partners' families socialized with backyard cookouts and dining out, and someday they hoped to plan a cruise with all of them away at the same time.

A cruise was the furthest thing from Peter's mind as he tried to focus on the spec sheet. The headache had shaken him. Was it connected to his malaise, or was this a separate situation to deal with? It was bad enough to suffer from depression. Peter was pragmatic enough to recognize his depression, but he hated the idea of seeking help, hoping it would pass.

"Hey there, Peter."

Startled, Peter looked up and discovered Bill Ebert standing at the opened door. He had a trim athletic build with sloping shoulders and a full head of wavy hair that tufted across his forehead. A member of the tennis team in college, he still played three times a week.

Then Tim Heiden entered and closed the door.

Peter faced his partners: preppy, jovial Bill and taciturn, roly-poly Tim. Peter extended a hand and said, "Have a seat, guys."

They sat in leather reception chairs facing Peter's desk.

Tim got right to the point and informed Peter of their concern about his recent lack of production. "We're still waiting for you to sign off on three spec sheets," he told Peter. He then went on with a list of other duties that Peter had shirked.

Then Peter's *mood* was brought up. "You have everyone around here on pins and needles," Tim told him.

Peter tried to tell them it was nothing and that he'd get back at it.

But Bill mentioned that his brother who suffered from depression and noted that Peter was exhibiting similar signs. "Sullen moods, lack of interest," Bill said. "I could go on and on."

Peter began to speak, but Tim cut him off. "Bill and I both agree that you need counseling."

"I won't see a shrink," Peter told them. "But I will set up an appointment with my physician." He looked at Tim and then at Bill. "All right?"

"For now," Tim said. "That's good, for now."

CHAPTER 3

Since his meeting with his partners a few weeks back, Peter had mustered the energy to complete a review of the three spec sheets Tim had mentioned, plus a final proposal. Part of his impetus was to get Tim off his back, who had been calling or dropping by Peter's office unannounced every other day for status updates.

Originally, Peter had had no intention of following through with a doctor's appointment, but the headaches had been arriving sporadically, sometimes a doozy with lingering nausea and dizziness. First the depression, and now these skull-rattling headaches. Were they related? Or were the headaches a symptom of something far more serious? His entire life had been thrown for a loop.

Peter's doctor, Bob Goodman, was a neighbor and a friend from years of playing horseshoes on Wednesday evenings in Bob's backyard with some neighborhood guys. Peter had posted only once this past summer. In the past, he had rarely missed the chance to forget about everything while drinking a few beers, clanging a shoe against an iron stake, and swapping off-color jokes.

In Dr. Goodman's examination room, the nurse instructed Peter to undress down to his underwear and have a seat on the examination table. Shortly afterward, Bob came in. He was a tall man in his late fifties, with a fit, angular build from many years of a variety of physical activities.

"Peter." Dr. Goodman placed a hand on his patient's shoulder and said, "Long time."

"Bob," Peter said in greeting as the doctor took a seat at a small desk in the corner. He took a minute to go over Peter's medical chart before looking up. "So what's this about headaches?"

"They started a couple of weeks ago. I never know when they are going to arrive or the severity. Some are pretty bad."

"Anything else?"

"I get two or three a week. Sometimes dizziness and nausea afterward, and I've been," Peter said through a sigh, "depressed for months." He threw his hands out. "I don't what the hell is going on with me, Bob."

The doctor stood. "Come over to the scale, and we'll get you measured and weighed."

Peter got on the scale, and Bob adjusted the measuring rod. "Well, you're the same height, five foot ten and a half."

Bob slid the sliding weight down the scale's weight beam. "You've gained ten pounds, 174."

"Yeah," Peter said. "I haven't been running lately."

Bob looked at Peter for a moment with an inquiring slant to his eyebrows, before motioning his patient back to the examination table. "Let's check you over, and then we'll do the blood work."

After a stethoscope exam of the throat and ears followed by breathe in, breathe out while tapping Peter's back, Bob examined each of Peter's fingers and toes. "All right, Peter, lie on your back." He ran his fingers over Peter's scalp as though searching for defects, and then the neck and shoulders.

The doctor ran his finger over a one-inch indentation on Peter's left side. "Huh," he said as he discovered a similar one on his hip. "They are like little contoured grooves imprinted on your skin. I never noticed these before."

"Oh, those … had them all my life," Peter said. "Deb calls them my mystery dimples. When we were first dating, they fascinated her, and she would touch them for good luck. She still likes to run her fingers over them when we're intimate."

"They are uniquely strange. Some ancient cultures consider natural body anomalies a carryover from a past life. But …" Bob smiled a thin, knowing smile and said, "you're too much a pragmatist to believe in the power of myth."

After the exam, Bob sat at the desk while Peter dressed. "Peter, I haven't seen you but once this year at horseshoes."

Peter slipped on his undershirt. "Like I said, Bob, I haven't felt right for some time now. I've been a jerk to everyone in my life I care for, and I can't seem to stop myself." He reached for his shirt and said, "I've gotten so bad my partners wanted me to see a shrink."

"What's it like at home?"

Peter stopped buttoning his shirt and looked at Bob, a man who every year traveled to a medical conference in a foreign land to absorb the culture. To Peter, he was an older, wiser man, a Renaissance-type guy with hobbies ranging from nineteenth-century English literature to archeology—a man Peter could trust.

"Home life is not good, Bob. I have rattled Deb, to the point that she is acting out of character, and Devon is having a rough freshman year in high school, and I am not helping one damn bit." Peter exchanged a quick glance with his physician.

"How so?"

"He's lost his friends at school to an in-crowd, and I suspect he's getting bullied." Peter took a breath to collect himself. "The boy has totally withdrawn to his bedroom, and I haven't done a damn thing to help him."

"Have you tried talking with him?"

Peter stepped into his trousers and said, "Once, and I did not try very hard." He tucked in his shirt and said, "I have no desire to do anything other than get through the day. It's like I'm missing a part of myself."

Bob sat facing Peter, arms folded across his chest, his expression saying, Go ahead. Get it all out.

"And," Peter said, "these damn, miserable headaches ... I go three days without one and think they're over, and then I get slammed."

"All right, Peter. Let's wait until we get your blood work back and go from there."

"Do you think there's a connection between these recent headaches and the mood change I've been experiencing for what seems forever?"

Dr. Goodman rested his knuckle under his chin and said, "When it comes to the human body, Peter, everything is related."

CHAPTER 4

During his time with Bob Goodman, Peter's spirits had risen. But now as he was driving alone in his car, the malaise filtered its way back, a general sense of what-the-hell draping him in lethargy. He was beginning to understand why depressed people took medication and drank to excess—anything to break the endless cycle of gripping ennui. And then throw in those disconcerting headaches.

Speak of the devil, Peter thought. He pulled off the road into a strip mall parking lot as a pulsating throb pounded his skull. In a back corner next to a Dumpster, he turned off the engine and gripped the steering wheel. He folded his arms across his chest, rocking back and forth as he let out an ear-shattering, "Agghh."

After fifteen minutes, he felt well enough to drive and decided to go home.

The house was empty. Deb was probably out running errands, and Devon was at school. He scoured the refrigerator more out of habit than hunger. Out the kitchen window, the hammock drew his attention. Often on Saturdays he had enjoyed a nap under the shade of the red oak after a long run. Prior to the onset of his malaise, Peter had run on weekends and when he had time during the week.

In high school, a buddy had talked him into joining the cross-country team. Peter had stopped running when he got to college but picked it back up a few years after and entered local 10- and 20Ks. It had been an integral part of his life for nearly twenty years, but now he had no desire, or more accurately, his body seemed not to have the energy to expend.

But the hammock did look inviting. *Why not?* he thought as he headed for the back door.

He started to get up on the hammock, but it was no use; sleep or relaxation was not an option. On the way back toward the house, he stopped at the observation platform.

Grandpa Rudy on his mother's side had introduced Peter to stargazing. The summer of his tenth year, Peter visited his grandparents' ranch in eastern Oregon. The first night the sky was clear, the moon just a sliver, and grandfather and grandson walked up a hill behind the barn. From their vantage point, the sight of the stars sparkling like a cluster of jewels in the black sky held young Peter Richards with more than just youthful curiosity … something that he could not put a name to.

Grandfather and grandson shared stargazing that first time with a pair of binoculars. Grandpa identified Venus, Mars, and Ursa Major. Young Peter had never considered this mysterious world beyond Mother Earth.

Soon after, every night before bed, he stargazed from a binocular stand on his bedroom windowsill.

He learned from a children's book on the constellations that the stars in the night sky were images from a long, long time ago, like ghosts from another world.

One cluster of stars, the Pleiades, drew him like no other. Those sparkling blue gems, high in the eastern sky with a cascade of stars trailing down from the dipper, shined so brightly on a clear night.

He even dreamed about them, alone in a dark sky, sometimes inverted … his upside-down dreams, he called them. When dreaming, he was immersed in the wonder of those luminous, mysterious stars.

Once awake, he gave it little thought. He never wondered about his fascination or his dreams; he just watched them. But like everything else important to him, he had been ignoring stargazing, even at the Pleiades.

Peter pulled down the retractable steps from under the platform and climbed up. He closed the trapdoor and went to the post-and-timber railing. It seemed strange standing up here in the middle of the day. The sky, a dull gray, offered little encouragement.

He saw Debra at the kitchen window. Their eyes locked for a moment. In her gaze, a glimmer of hope flickered behind a deep shadow of worry—hope that he would come around and worry that he wouldn't. He wanted desperately to raise a hand to let her know everything was going to be okay, that he still loved her as much as their first time camping together, and he knew she was the one. But he did no such thing.

That pull of love toward her was still in him, but an internal barrier had come between them, a barrier that he could not see and could barely comprehend.

* * *

Three days after his initial exam, Peter sat across a double-pedestal mahogany desk from Bob Goodman. It dawned on him that this was his first time in the doctor's office. Pictures of Bob and his wife in exotic locales hung on the wall behind Bob. Below each photograph was a brief description: Hiking Aoraki, Mt. Cook, New Zealand ... Shamwari Game Reserve, South Africa ... Taj Mahal, Agra, India. In each photo Bob's expression was not that of a tourist but of a confident man immersed in the culture, the gaze steady and sure, shoulders straight, and a toothy smile of one on a great adventure.

Dr. Bob Goodman closed a folder he had been scanning and looked up at Peter. "Everything is normal." His eyes, dark blue and heavy-lidded, took in Peter with calm appraisal.

"Well, maybe these headaches and dizzy spells are just stress from work."

Bob shrugged *maybe*, but his eyes said probably not. "Just to be safe, let's get an MRI."

"Really?"

"Peter, we need to discover the root of the problem," Bob explained. "There are various possibilities."

"Okay, what next?"

"I am sending you to a neurologist."

A quiver like a thousand tiny pinpricks jangled down Peter's spine. "A neurologist?"

Back at work, Peter examined the schematic design for a proposal. This had been Peter's wheelhouse where a written concept was transformed into a spatial reality. He had an innate ability to design people's ideas for a home or building and sketch out what they pictured in their mind. The project was a reclamation of an abandoned factory that the clients wanted to transform into a hotel, while saving as much of the integrity of the original building as possible.

To take something ruined and re-create it into a useful structure was normally the type of project that Peter went at with zeal. Now he had to force himself to concentrate on the dimensions.

When they first started the firm, he would write out a rough draft proposal that included the project scope with schematic designs, phases from groundbreaking to final detail, compensation, and schedule of payments. Then he would have Debra edit to make sure there were no grammatical errors, making her feel a part of his career.

After the final proposal was accepted, he would arrive home hiding a bottle of champagne behind his back, announcing to Debra, "Well, we just signed another one." He'd place the bottle on the kitchen table. "Take off your apron, Deb. I am cooking steaks on the grill."

It became a routine where Debra would see the hand behind the back and begin taking off her apron before he could make his announcement. Once Peter fooled her when he revealed an empty hand, and her face had taken on a look of head-scratching bemusement. She stood there waiting, knowing that he had something else up his sleeve. And well he did, for he had signed a large high-rise. Peter told her they were going to celebrate with his partners and their wives at one of the best restaurants in town.

But those days were no more; each segment of the project was no longer a pleasure but a task to complete and be done with.

Peter got up from his desk and went to the window. A recent dry spell had left the Wycee Creek only a trickle. Spanning the creek was a batten-board bridge that Peter had designed gratis for the Multnomah County Planning Commission. It was a lovely little bridge with a camber arch and a set of stone pilasters standing guard at each entrance. Also, he had drawn the plans for converting the woodland across the creek into an elliptical green crisscrossed by walks intersecting at a wishing-well fountain. Native Oregon spruce and cedar trees had been planted around the park's perimeter, and crab apples, dogwoods, and shrubs were located strategically inside the space to maintain the open atmosphere. There was something reassuring about being able to stand at his window and look down upon his creation.

The park was empty. He checked the sun's position in the sky—a skill his grandfather had taught him as a boy—and calculated the time at 11:40 a.m.

This was the first day he could remember the old gentleman not in his seat, facing the fountain, with book in hand. Nothing seemed to be going right—not even the one thing left that he still looked forward to.

Why did an old man sitting on a park bench provide pleasure? The fact that he had designed the park was partly it, but it was more than that. It was the way a crippled elderly man, who seemed all alone, still got up every day. Not the best or easiest or most enjoyable life, but he had the courage to see it through.

Peter decided to try to finish a draft of the proposal for Debra to edit. It would be a little sign to her that he was trying to return to his old self.

Some of the exterior elevations and locations of the closets were not to Peter's liking. He tried to picture the adjustments, but his mind drew a blank. He could not possibly finish. He could plod his way through it, yes, but there was no way in his present condition he could complete today what a year ago he would have done with time to spare.

He told himself it was because he was concerned about having to see a neurologist, nothing more. And once this headache thing was taken care, he'd be back on top of his game. He had convinced himself that the headaches were connected to his malaise. He liked the word *malaise*, which, according to the dictionary, was a mild sickness—just a temporary setback. He could solve the headache problem and the malaise would disappear, and he would be back in his prime grinding away on some project, geometric objects floating in his spatial imagination finding their proper places as he designed his creation. What a feeling of utter control and power he got from times like that. But deep down below his false front was the nagging question, would he ever feel that way again?

* * *

From the kitchen window, Peter saw Debra in the vegetable garden in the rear corner of the backyard. He had designed and built the garden with one-fourth-by-six-inch cedar planks for the raised beds that he assembled with slots and pegs. The design was not his but from the seventeenth century. He had found it in a book on the history of English gardening that he bought for one dollar at a yard sale.

By the second year, Deb had joined him. Every spring they weeded, spread compost from their own pile of kitchen scraps and yard trimmings, and planted. It was a chore they had always enjoyed, but this year Peter had fizzled out.

As Debra weeded a bed clustered with tomato plants bulging with fat beefeaters, Peter approached her rear and said hi.

She straightened up and looked over her shoulder with a twist of her neck. "Peter, I didn't hear you coming."

"Something I need to tell you."

Debra removed her gardening gloves and flicked strands of hair off her forehead. "Yes, what is it?"

"I've been having pretty bad headaches lately and finally went to see Bob Goodman." Peter paused expecting some comment but was met by silence. "Anyway, I had a physical and everything was fine, but Bob has set up an appointment with a neurologist."

Debra squinted trying to comprehend, the corner of her mouth twisting in a downward slant. "What does Bob—"

"Says it could be many things. It's probably nothing."

"Oh, Peter," Debra said. "How long has this been going on?"

"Around three weeks."

"Three weeks?" She looked at Peter, her expression of one who had suffered a body blow.

A swirl of emotion caught in Peter's throat as he realized the distance to which his relationship with Debra had fallen. He wanted to scream out that he believed it was related to his mood, but he could not do it, would not do it, for that inner barrier kept him from connecting with his wife. Instead, Peter shrugged and said, "Bob thinks the MRI may reveal something."

Debra rested her elbow on her forearm across her waist and brought her hand under her chin, her eyes questioning her husband. "So, did you talk to Bob about," she said, raising an eyebrow with an inquiring slant, "your mood?"

"Yes."

"And?"

"I talked, he listened."

Debra put her hands on her hips as if ready for come what may. "I don't understand all that's going on with you, Peter."

"I know that." Peter wanted to wrap his arms around that good woman, holding her tight. But that inner wall in him said, no go.

Debra looked at Peter waiting, waiting for him to say something, anything. But he remained silent. She put her gloves back on and returned to her garden.

Back in the kitchen, Peter poured himself a glass of water from the tap and then poured it out. He went over to the five-gallon ceramic water jug stationed on a stained oak stand that he had built. A few years back he had read an article on the impurities of tap water and the potential for lead to infiltrate a water system. After researching the subject, he decided on buying purified water from a local company.

Debra was skeptical of Devon drinking water without fluoride, but she went along with it, though occasionally he would catch her drinking water from the tap. "Deb," he once said in mock horror, "don't let our child see you sneaking your fluoride fix." They both had a good laugh about it.

Then one day he read a newspaper article about rusty public water pipes accompanied with pictures. He showed it to Debra, who was taken aback by the scaly corrosion. After that, she was as much a believer as Peter.

At the kitchen table, he sipped his purified water, wondering what in the world was going on with himself. It seemed that a stranger had entered his body, a confused, disinterested entity.

Peter heard the front door open and saw Devon plod his way into the kitchen. There was a lost-boy look about his son that said, I am miserable.

"Hi, Dev," Peter said, trying hard to sound interested. "How'd your day go?"

Devon plopped his knapsack on the table and said, "Okay." He took a glass from the cabinet and went to the water jug. He then picked up his knapsack and went into his room, closing the door behind him.

As Peter considered a heart-to-heart with his son, he felt the first throb of a headache and thought, *Oh no, not here.* He went through the den to the side door, under the breezeway to the garage, and locked the door.

It had been weeks since he had entered his workshop. It held too many memories of his old self cutting wood on the ripsaw, routing, drilling holes on the drill press, sanding, finishing. Every tool from hammer to tap-and-die set hung on the walls, and metal cabinets were filled with accessories and drawers of nuts, bolts, and screws of all shapes and sizes. It was his little castle where he did it his way. There were no clients to please, just Peter Richards building off his designs, such as his desk at work, the observation platform, the water-jug stand, the raised garden beds, and so many other projects that he had made with his mind and hands working in unison. What a beautiful feeling. But there was nothing beautiful about the stabbing relentless pain in his head that forced him into a fetal position on the concrete floor.

After the throbbing subsided, the nausea arrived. He went out the garage door to the side of the house. Behind a shrub, he bent over and began vomiting.

When he finished, he sat back against the house, knees bent against his chest. He wiped his watery eyes with the back of his hand. His cheek felt cold as though the blood had been drawn from his face.

Like a thunderbolt it struck him—this was serious, damn serious.

* * *

The week leading up to the neurological exam, Peter tried to apply himself at work and be there at home for his family. But he failed miserably at both as he continued to go through the motions. He went to work each day with good intentions but constantly had to remind himself to concentrate. He had three headaches, all at work. During the first he closed the office door and rode it out. The next two, he got the key to the bathroom from Dory and hid out in a stall until the all clear. After the last one, when he returned the key to Dory, she asked if he was all right. He told her he was fine but knew she didn't buy it. He imagined he looked as shaky as he felt.

At home, he half-watched TV in the den while Devon stayed in his room with the door closed, leaving Debra to fend for herself. It was almost as though they were three boarders living under one roof, all going their own way.

Dinner, their only time together, was spent in silence, except when Deb tried to break the ice about an innocuous subject such as the weather or the garden. She would be met with blank stares or at best a nod from

Peter. One time he did begin a conversation before his voice trailed off as he waved his hand to indicate never mind.

After the neurological exam, Peter had an MRI and a spinal tap the following week at the hospital. He could get nothing out of the neurologist other than, "Need the results. Call you when I get them."

During this period, his life had evolved into a repetitive series of events as though he was climbing a long flight of steps, never getting to the top and starting each day anew at the bottom tread, wondering if and when a headache would hit.

At last, Peter got the call at work and drove straight to the neurologist's office. He waited an excruciating twenty minutes in the reception area before he was taken to the doctor's private office. Then he waited another ten minutes before the doctor entered. He was a gawky, lank man with thin lips and sharp, bony features that even his starched white lab coat could not hide.

He squinted a hello and took a seat at his desk facing Peter. "You have a malignant tumor in your brain. So far the rest of your body is clear." His tone was flat and cold.

Peter felt a knee-shaking jolt of fear ransack his body.

"You need to see a surgeon to assess what your options are."

Options? Peter gathered himself and said, "What are my chances?"

"Hard for me to say."

Again, the flatness in the man's voice sent little shock waves through Peter. Did the bastard even care?

Shaken to his core, Peter sat in his car in the medical-center parking lot. A numbing void engulfed his mind before the reality of the situation jolted him back. He needed to collect himself.

As he often did, he looked over his surroundings with his architect's eye. The parking lot was divided into sections, one after another dotted around sleek, shiny buildings of glass and steel without a tree or a strip of grass in sight. It fit the neurologist perfectly—cold, unemotional, uncaring.

He needed Dr. Bob Goodman, not only as a physician but as a friend. Peter called Bob's office from his cell phone, but he was out of the country at a medical convention in Singapore, of all places. Bob had left a surgeon's name, a Dr. Porten, as if he had expected the news of a tumor. His staff made an appointment.

On the way home, a monster headache struck. Peter barely managed to pull off the freeway into the parking lot of an abandoned warehouse. As his head pounded, he bent forward head in his hands, groaning. After ten minutes the pain subsided, but his stomach was queasy. Outside the car with hands on his knees, a series of retching dry heaves left him emotionally shaken. He straightened up, and before him the old warehouse loomed. It was a desolate, crumbling brick structure probably built back in the twenties. Graffiti and broken windows were further indications that this place from another time had run its course.

Much like Peter, its fate was in the hands of others. He imagined that the dilapidated building was handsome in its day. The external dark-red brick masonry appeared load-bearing, probably timber joist or maybe wrought-iron beams. The windows were recessed Venetian style and, even in disrepair, there was a lingering beauty to them. They didn't make warehouses like this anymore.

With the right team, this old building could be rebuilt to its former stature and once again be useful, maybe with green growth in mind by salvaging the bricks ... solar paneling and a roof with a garden. Yes, it was on its last legs, but the damage from time and neglect man could rebuild, making it stronger than before, offering it new life. Could Peter find someone to offer him new life?

* * *

No one was home. Peter considered calling Deb on her cell, but he wanted to tell her in person. He made a sandwich and sat at the kitchen table. The front door swung open, Devon coming in from school. "Hi, Dev."

The boy glanced at his father with a question in his eyes: What are you doing home early again? He took a glass from the cupboard.

"You know where your mother is?"

Devon looked at his father, trying to ascertain what was up. "Said she had errands and would be home by four," he said as he filled his glass from the water jug.

A voice in Peter's head told him to ask Devon about going out back to stargaze tonight, but much like with his relationship with Debra, he could not get the words out. Was this tumor causing his malaise? Oh, how he wished Bob Goodman were available. He could imagine Bob's answer:

"Yes, in some cases there is a correlation, Peter, but let's wait until you talk with the surgeon and we will go from there. Meantime, try and keep your spirits up, especially at home."

Devon grabbed his backpack, ignoring his father's eye contact.

"Homework?" Peter asked as he cut his sandwich diagonally.

"Yeah," Devon said, "homework."

The click of his son's bedroom door shutting seemed so benign and soft yet so terribly sad. Still, Peter had not the wherewithal or whatever it was this tumor was taking from him to do anything about it. He put away his untouched sandwich, went into the den, and stretched out on the sofa to wait for Debra.

The sound of Debra's car pulling into the driveway woke Peter from a half-asleep, half-awake nap. He greeted her at the front door. "Need to talk, Deb." He stepped out on the front stoop, closing the door. "I have a malignant brain tumor."

Debra dropped the bag of groceries, its glass contents breaking in a shattering pop. She took a step back and brought her hand to her mouth, which gaped open. Her eyes narrowed, searching Peter's face for any trace of good news. "What does that mean?"

"It means I am going to see a surgeon next Friday to find out what my options are."

"Options? Oh, my God, Peter." She looked at her husband as if not wanting to believe what she was hearing. "What did Bob say?"

"He's out of the country—won't be back until next week. His office arranged the appointment with the surgeon."

"Oh, Peter, what do we tell Dev?"

"Let's wait until after I see the surgeon."

CHAPTER 5

After the longest week of Peter Richard's life, Friday arrived. He did not wait long in an examination room before Dr. Porten came in holding an oversized hanging folder. Something about the folder seemed ominous.

The surgeon removed an x-ray and clipped it on a photo board on the wall. He turned around to face his patient, and in that instant their eyes met, Peter knew his worst fears were to become a reality.

"I am afraid I have bad news, Mr. Richards. The tumor is lodged in your cortex. It is inoperable."

Until that moment, Peter Richards never realized the power of words, no matter how softly and kindly they were said. The words had a ring of sorrow to them as opposed to the neurologist's brusque manner. But in the end, this man's style changed nothing. If the neurologist had delivered the news, Peter could not possibly have been any more or less affected.

As those deadly, final words, "I am afraid it's inoperable," echoed in his mind, Peter tried to concentrate as Dr. Porten placed the plastic tip of the wooden pointer on a vague gray spot on the x-ray of his skull. How small and insignificant that little spot appeared, as if one could rub it out with a finger to begin life anew.

"Glioblastoma multi …" the surgeon's voice trailed off as Peter's mind seemed to have entered a surreal dream gone horribly wrong.

Dr. Porten looked over his shoulder at Peter, his soft, round face radiating sympathy. This man was the polar opposite of the robotic neurologist, whose name Peter could no longer recall. Dr. Porten was short with none of the sharp features of the lank in the starched white lab coat, everything rounded off from the shoulders down to his squatty legs. "You won't start feeling the serious effects for a couple of months yet.

You have the options of chemo, radiation, drugs for pain, and I strongly recommend a cancer clinic."

Chemo? Radiation? Drugs? Cancer clinic? What frightening words. Peter hated all of these *options*, which would alter his chemistry, allowing painful side effects. How could this all be? How could he be facing death at age forty-four? What would become of Debra and Devon?

"I would like to get a second opinion." Peter heard the desperation in his voice.

"Of course," Dr. Porten said. "I or Dr. Goodman can recommend someone."

Peter knew Bob was still out of the country. "Do you know someone I can see today?"

"Today?" Dr. Porten looked kindly upon Peter and said, "Let me see if one of my partners can fit you in."

After a two-hour wait, Peter got his second opinion. It was the same as the first, inoperable.

Peter called Bob Goodman's office, and they set up an interview at a cancer clinic for Wednesday of next week.

On the ride home, Peter drove on automatic pilot, his mind in a fog. He needed to talk to Deb desperately. Did he have it in him to tell her how sorry he was for everything? And Devon … how would he ever tell his son, his only child, that he was going to die? He had to make the best out of what time he had left for both their sakes. Mingled with his malaise was a desperate state of remorse for the way he had acted of late. He must snap out of it.

Driving up to the entrance to Hemlock Hills, Peter noted that the ivy had been sheared off the brick wall. He hadn't attended a community meeting in some time. An image flashed in his mind of the old woman banging her cane on the floor and shaking it at the committee until she had gotten her wish. If he had been there, would he have tried to dissuade the committee? It didn't really matter, for the ivy was gone.

He got out of the car to investigate. The roots were still in the ground with a few leaves clinging on. Bits of decayed adhesive disks that attached the ivy still dug into the mortar. Peter had seen this before on a couple of projects; the disks form a humic acid that dissolves the mortar. The thick cover of ivy that had blanketed the wall had nearly destroyed it—too much of a good thing.

The wall would have to be thoroughly cleansed with an acid wash, cleaned and rinsed, and remortared. It would take two men a week to complete. But in the end the wall would once again be strong.

He parked in his driveway and turned off the engine. There was no sound but that dull, opaque hum in his ears—no birds chirping, no distant growl of a lawn mower or the drone of an airplane overhead … silence all around. Peter was about to do the hardest thing in this life: tell his family he was going to die. He closed his eyes and ran his hands over his face. How could this be happening?

He noted the barren lilac bush, its flowers long departed last spring. Would he be around next year to enjoy its lavender blooms?

When they first moved in, Peter had decided to draw up a landscape design for the yard. Debra requested a lilac to be located toward the front and with a stone border around the bed to highlight it. "I know it's only a short time that the lilac will bloom, but when it does, it is the most beautiful of things."

That first year it had bloomed for two full weeks, and she had been right—it was the most beautiful of things. Neighbors would stop on a walk to admire it while basking in the lovely fragrance from its vibrant clusters of elegant flowers.

One year, Peter found Debra collecting all the fallen leaves under the lilac. She told him she could not stand the sight of them fading away. She ran a finger softly over a leaf in her palm. "It is best to remember them when they shine so gloriously in the sunlight."

Peter turned his gaze to the ivy along the front walk, which he had finally gotten around to trimming, and he promised himself to stay on top of his yard and garden.

He had an image of the ivy roots deep in the soil at the base of the wall at the entrance, lying in wait until the time came and then springing back to life, once again covering the brick in a regal green shawl. Yes, one way or another, Peter told himself, the ivy would find a way.

Standing outside the car, Peter's turned his gaze to the empty window box under the bay window outside the den and noted that on the ground, snapdragon volunteers were sprouting. Their blooms of red and white brought to mind little patriots rallying for one last stand before the winter.

As Peter reached for the front door to the house, Debra opened it, her eyes raking his face for any good sign. He knew he should hug her, but his death sentence weighed like an anchor around his neck. What the hell was wrong with him?

"Let's talk in the kitchen, Deb," Peter said in a tone indicating more bad news.

Debra stared at Peter, her eyes like those of a deer caught in the headlights. "Okay," she said in a raspy whisper.

Peter sat with his elbows on the kitchen table, his chin resting on folded hands. "I have maybe a year."

"Oh, Peter."

"Dr. Porten, the first surgeon, and a partner both said surgery is not an option. The tumor is too close to the cortex."

"Dr. Porten?" A question hung on her bottom lip, her stunned eyes staring across the table at her husband. She tried to speak but managed only a meager grunt.

There was a moment of silence before Peter brought his folded hands down onto the table and said, "I am going to check out a cancer clinic on Wednesday. I want to wait before we tell Dev."

"We have to tell him, Peter."

"I know, just not yet." They exchanged glances, and Peter said, "The second surgeon mentioned that mental instability is possible with my type of cancer." He ran his index finger along a circular grain on the tabletop. "Might explain some things."

Debra reached her hand across the table, placing it on top of Peter's. "Tell me about the cancer clinic."

* * *

Peter's appointment at the cancer clinic was with Dr. Ellen Granger. The clinic was a separate wing at a local hospital. The place had that ammonia hospital smell of sterile cleanliness, too much cleanliness. He waited in a reception area with other people who he assumed were all in various stages of cancer treatment. Some appeared in good health while others were in varying degrees of decline.

One man in a wheelchair was thin to the point of looking near starvation. His withered, gray face looked to belong on a cadaver, and a prominent Adam's apple bulged nearly as thick as his pencil neck. A woman who appeared to be his wife stood at his side.

Then it struck Peter that these folks lived in his neighborhood. He didn't know them other than passing by in the car as they walked vigorously together in the evening. He assumed that they were recently retired, in their late sixties. He hadn't seen them for some time now and was shocked at how they both had aged. There were dark circles under the wife's eyes, which had that vacant look of one in need of sleep, and stamped on her face was an expression of utter despair. And her hair seemed to have turned white overnight.

The woman caught Peter looking at them. There was a desperateness about her, like that of a wild animal caught in a trap with no chance of escape. He wondered whether the man had resisted coming until his wife couldn't take it any longer.

A nurse escorted Peter to an office where a woman dressed in a lab coat sat at a desk. Dr. Ellen Granger was thin with dark, intelligent eyes and an assured air.

She explained to Peter that the clinic had a multitude of treatments, depending on the patient's condition. "My condition," Peter said, "is terminal."

A thin smile creased her lips. "Yes, I am aware of that, Mr. Richards." The smile widened like that of an actress on cue. "Our job here is to make your quality of life as comforting and uplifting as possible." She then proceeded to tell Peter about medications to alleviate discomfort.

Peter asked whether his mood was related to the cancer, but she was noncommittal. She went over therapy classes to maintain mobility for as long as possible, group workshops with other patients, and in the later stages, hospice facilities at the clinic.

Never had Peter felt so damn low as while Dr. Granger presented her spiel. My God, what a way to go. What a place to die in … slowly decaying in this stark white institution with wards that Peter imagined smelled of death.

He told the doctor that he wanted to discuss it with his wife. "Of course," she replied.

He then asked if he could look around the facility. She folded her hands together on her desk and said, "We can arrange for a tour, if you'd like." Her tone was careful as if she was hiding something. *Patients toward the end of the road,* Peter thought.

Back home, Peter told Deb about his meeting with Dr. Granger. She looked across the kitchen table and asked, "Are you going to go there?"

"Don't like the place, but I don't have many options. There was a man there in the later stages of his illness. His wife was with him. I would not want you to end up in her condition." Peter reached across the table and held his wife's hand. "I will do anything to prevent that."

The creak of the front door opening broke the moment.

Devon entered the kitchen to find his parents in the middle of the day at the kitchen table. He stared at the unusual scene before him. "What's going on?"

"Let's go in the den, Dev," Peter said.

Peter sat on the sofa under the front bay window. Shadows, cast indiscriminately by waning sunlight, filtered into the room.

Devon stood squinting at his father. Little alarms seemed to go off in his eyes. "Dad, what is it?"

Peter glanced at Debra standing in the doorway behind Devon.

"Dad, please. What's going on?"

"I've been diagnosed with brain cancer and have been given no more than a year to live."

The boy's eyes seemed ready to spring from their sockets. "What?"

"I wish it were not so, Dev, but it is."

Devon shook his head as though not wanting to believe what he had heard.

Peter stood, reaching for his son, who pushed him away. Devon rocked back on his heels and whirled away from his father, storming past his mother.

Debra looked at Peter, her gaze that of an innocent bystander witnessing a tragedy. Their world was coming apart. He went to her, wrapping his arms around her, the scent of Deb's soft-as-rainwater hair in his nostrils.

As the last bit of sunlight faded from the room, Peter and Debra stood numb in the shadows.

CHAPTER 6

The following morning, Peter arrived at work early. From his office window he watched employees filter in. Finally, Tim showed, and then shortly after, Bill.

He waited ten minutes and then phoned his partners.

When they arrived, Peter told Dory no interruptions. Bill started a conversation about his tennis game, and Peter cut him off with a raised hand. "Excuse me."

Bill stopped in the middle of mimicking his overhead stroke.

An *uh-oh* moment hung in the air.

Peter said, "I've been diagnosed with brain cancer and have no more than a year to live."

After much sympathy and concern from his partners, Peter then broke the news to Dory and his staff. The looks on their faces made it seem he was witnessing his own funeral. He also apologized for the way he had been acting of late.

While Peter was cleaning out his desk, Dory peeked in. "I'll be saying rosary for you every Sunday at Mass, Peter."

Peter looked up from a cardboard box on his desk filled with personal mementos. "I could not have had a better assistant." He placed his hand across his chest. "Thank you for always being there for me, Dory." He tapped his chest twice over his heart. "I am truly sorry for the way I have treated you lately."

Dory cleared her throat quietly and said, "Not to worry, Peter, not to worry." She stole once last glance at her boss, turned from him, and returned to her desk.

Peter went to the window. It had been a while since he had seen the old gentleman at his park bench. A premonition told him he would not be back. Some would consider it an omen, a metaphysical signpost—the disappearance of the old man.

After storing the box of mementos in the backseat of his car, Peter walked over to the pedestrian bridge for one last look. He ran his hand on one of the stone pilasters. The trickle of the water drew his gaze to a rivulet gurgling along the nearly empty streambed. He had never seen it so low. But it was only a matter of time before it would be flowing again. This old creek could endure a drought and come back stronger than ever.

In the middle of the batten-board deck, he bent down and ran his fingers over a bronze plate screwed into the middle of the deck, which acknowledged Peter's contribution. As he stood back up, he realized there was one more thing he needed to do.

He sat on a bench, not any bench, but the one that the elderly man had sat on every day with his sandwich and book.

Peter leaned forward, forearms on thighs, and laced his fingers together. He felt a twinge of sadness for the old gent, but also a bit of jealousy that the man had lived a full life … maybe not a happy life but a long one. Now Peter was getting shortchanged. It wasn't fair, dammit. He wished there was an alternative to radiation, chemo, drugs, and that god-awful cancer clinic. He had a friend from college who, a few years back, received radiation and chemo for colon cancer and went from a strapping 200 pounds to 120. His once-keen mind disintegrated to senility, and before his death, he was a broken-down old man.

He didn't want to go out that way, but what choice did he have? Something in his gut nagged at him, though. He needed to talk with Bob Goodman. He needed to hear from that old soul. Yes, Bob Goodman was the man to talk to if only to lift Peter's spirit. He was to return from Singapore the day after tomorrow. Meanwhile, Peter needed to put back together at home what had come apart.

Ever since the diagnosis was confirmed by the second surgeon, a slow but perceptible difference had filtered into his psyche. He wasn't his old self, but the sullen grip of despondency had slackened. And seeping into his core was the will to rally against this terrible cancer, to fight back like the decimated ivy on the brick wall.

The first sign was when he had reached across the kitchen table for Debra's hand, saying he would do anything to prevent her from ending up like the wife of the dying man at the cancer clinic. And then he had wrapped his arms around Deb for the first time in months. Could the fact that he now knew his condition have changed his outlook? There were so many things to discuss with Bob.

Peter stood and looked around. It struck him that *after*, his park and bridge would still be here. For years to come people would enjoy his creation, and another regular visitor like the old man might seek solace among its solitude and beauty.

* * *

Inching along in freeway traffic, Peter felt a throbbing like a mallet pounding the inside of his head. He had made a promise to avoid the freeway for just this reason, but in his hazy state he forgot. Fortunately, an exit ramp was ahead. He parked in the same warehouse parking lot as last week.

After ten minutes, the pain abated but with a residue of dizziness. At least there was no nausea. He decided to take a closer look at the warehouse, one step at a time, staying vigilant not to stumble from his light-headedness.

Many people would consider this structure mundane and ugly with its irregularly shaped bricks and rectangular shape, ignoring the fine details of recessed Venetian windows that Peter had previously noted. But he had missed the fluted pilaster at the double-door entrance and the detailed cornices along the roofline.

In his mind's eye he saw it back in its day, beauty in simplicity of form combined with detailed craftsmanship.

A few years back, a client had wanted a fire-damaged mansion reconstructed with a weathered brick façade in an 1890s Victorian style with turrets, gables, and arched Palladian windows with dentil molding. Peter had drawn up the plans with a façade of clinker bricks, much like those on the warehouse before him. He had found a brick-collecting company that had the old bricks in stock. The finished product blended Old World charm with energy efficiency, a lighting-control system, and geothermal heat pumps. Every so often he pictured in his mind the reclamation that he had played a large part in bringing back to life.

Out of the corner of his eye, Peter saw a red-flagged survey stake at the corner of the building, and at the other end he saw another one.

He ran his palm over the rough, worn façade. Would it be rebuilt from scratch, shiny and sleek? Or would the remains be integrated into the new design? He could only hope that these fine old bricks would find a home, if not here, somewhere.

Back in the car, Peter needed a minute before driving. He turned the radio to a local afternoon talk show he tuned in to on occasion. Half-listening, he put the car in drive and then stopped when the guest voice said, "I was given no more than a year to live." Peter turned up the volume as the man continued, "I had a rare blood disorder that there was no known cure for. I was handed my walking papers."

The voice had a cadence that spoke in clusters of words and then a pause. Peter guessed this was a no-nonsense person, not one easily led on wild-goose chases, but giving chase when one's life was at stake.

"I had nothing to lose, and a friend who had recently returned from Peru told me about a shaman in the Andes who had the power to heal. I did some research and flew to Peru. A guide took me on a journey to the Andean village of Abrreara, where an old man named Concho …"

It passed briefly in Peter's mind that his dizziness had left, and in its place was a surge of energy.

During a commercial break, Peter reflected on how horribly cancer treatment had affected his friend and the skeleton-like neighbor at the cancer clinic with his distraught, haggard wife.

As the show resumed, the host caught new listeners up to the gist of the topic and then asked the guest to continue. "I lived in a mountain village for a week and took the shaman's medicinal cure of leaves and potions. I returned home with a clean bill of health, to the amazement of my doctors. I have letters of proof here from my physician who …"

* * *

Finally, Bob Goodman was back. He wasn't at work but had returned home yesterday from his trip.

"Bob, Peter here."

"Yes, Peter, how are you? I did call the office today and found out about your results."

"Look, Bob, that's why I called. I have a favor to ask. Are you free tonight around six?"

Bob Goodman's backyard was a wide swath of lush green grass with an English garden in the middle surrounded by a freshly painted white picket fence bordering its perimeter and a smattering of trees about the yard. The bare-ground horseshoe pits with two iron rods set forty feet apart in the ground were under a vase-shaped, stately American elm, its crown with an array of splaying branches growing and bending in many different directions. Peter had always thought the tree to be a perfect metaphor for Bob.

Bob and Peter stood on each side of the pit closest to the house. Bob, with fingers wrapped around one of the shanks of the horseshoe and eyes on the target, rocked his left arm back, stepped forward, and released the shoe with a flick of his wrist. The shoe lazily floated in the air in one complete revolution, landing past the pin. "Been doing any stargazing lately, Peter?"

"No, I lost interest with all that's been going on."

Bob flicked a clump of dirt off a shoe. "A big astrological event is coming." He looked at Peter and said, "The Pleiades, Peter, that mysterious cluster of stars."

Peter glanced sideways at Bob as if to say, Is there anything you don't know? "I had forgotten."

Bob tossed another shoe, a leaner. "Maybe you and Devon could stargaze together."

"You're right, Bob. I should, but I am having trouble connecting with him. On top of everything else, he didn't take my cancer well."

"Anytime Devon comes in for a checkup or whatnot, we talk about the stars." A breeze picked up, ruffling the branches high in the big elm. Bob turned his gaze from the tree to Peter. "I cannot think of a better way to reconnect with your son." Bob tossed his last shoe, and it clanged down on the leaner for a double ringer.

"Good idea, Bob," Peter said as he tossed his first shoe short of the ring. "I went to the cancer clinic the other day." Peter looked at Bob for a reaction but was met by an expression of calm appraisal. "The place depressed the hell out of me."

Bob let out a wry laugh. "Depressed?" he said. "That's been your modus operandi of late."

Peter shrugged and said, "You got me there, Bob." He tossed his shoe, clanging it off the side of the ring onto the hard-packed dirt. "I saw one couple there that I cannot get out of my mind, people I would see walking in the neighborhood. The man was in a wheelchair—looked near death. But his wife looked even worse. They appeared to have aged in dog years."

Bob nodded at Peter, his eyes looking kindly on his patient and friend. "Yes, it can be a difficult situation."

"That's why I am resisting going there. I would be going there to die." Peter threw his last shoe, a perfect ringer that clanged atop Bob's two rings. "All right," he said before shooting a glance at Bob. "What do you know about shamans?"

Bob looked at Peter as though not believing what he'd heard. "Of all the people to ask me about shamans, you would have been the last. I could give you the song-and-dance pep talk about radiation and chemo and all the rest of it, but the truth is that it will be prolonged agony ending with death." Bob reached into a Styrofoam cooler and pulled out two ice-cold cans of beer. He popped them both open and handed one to Peter. "As your friend and doctor, I think alternative treatment is an option to be considered."

"Before all this I would never have bought into any of it, but I've seen a good friend die a slow, horrible death from cancer. And the treatment he received made the entire process agonizing to watch."

Bob took a long swallow of his beer and circled his finger three times around the rim. "What if I told you I have a colleague, an internist, who had a patient with a rare form of cancer who was given six months to a year." He looked up into the dusky sky, the gray outline of the half moon now visible. "He went off to Mongolia and found a shaman who cured him. I saw the x-rays before and after the patient returned." Bob looked at Peter and said, "The cancer was gone."

Peter took a swig of his beer. He exchanged a glance with Bob and then looked up at the moon, which was either waxing or waning. Normally he would know which, but now he wasn't sure.

Bob said, "Peter, I can't promise you any miracles, but I have studied this subject. I have some papers I would like you to read and some websites to check out."

* * *

Clutching a packet of articles and papers on shamans, Peter stood on his front stoop to collect himself. It seemed as though an engine had been turned on powering not only his body but his mind, and with it came hope.

But the pragmatic realist in him stifled this emerging wave of optimism. *Are you crazy, running off to some foreign land in search of a witch doctor? What do you do when the headaches get worse? And what would this do to your family? Is it not better to die here with them, rather than far away and alone chasing some wild-eyed fantasy? Spend the time you have left with Deb and Devon.*

All so rationally true, but what was there to lose in reading Bob's literature and researching shamans online? He needed a respite from dwelling on the cancer clinic, and along with it was that nagging sensation deep below the surface that pushed him to seek out the road less traveled.

Peter reached for the door and held it for a moment. He wouldn't tell Debra about his conversation with Bob on shamanism. Why not read the material, and then if he still found it feasible, talk it over with her?

But first, there was one thing he needed to do.

Peter knocked on his son's bedroom door and peeked in. "Got a minute, Dev?"

Devon shrugged his shoulders—whatever.

Peter sat on the edge of the bed facing his son's profile. "How are things going?"

"Fine." Devon's gaze remained on an open book.

"The first year of high school can be tough. People you thought were one way change."

Devon kept staring at his book, his expression that of distressed detachment.

Where have I been? Peter thought. "I want you to know that I am here if you want to talk."

"About what?"

"Anything, Dev."

"I'm okay."

Devon's toneless voice tugged at Peter as he stood and went to his son's side.

The boy glanced up at his father and then looked straight ahead. "What's there to talk about? You're going to die."

Peter put his hand on his son's shoulder, and Devon leaned away. "Dev, look at me. Please, look at me."

The boy stared point-blank at his father, as if Peter were a stranger on the street asking for directions.

Peter reached for the astronomy book resting on the corner of the desk. He opened it to a picture of the Pleiades and placed it in front of Devon. "A big event is coming soon."

Devon looked at the picture and then at his father. "What's that?"

"In a couple of days, the moon is occulting the Pleiades."

Devon stayed silent for a moment and then said, "Oh, yeah."

"What do you say we get the telescope out for the big event?"

Devon looked at his father, and in his son's gaze, Peter saw a glimmer like the first crack of light at dawn.

Later that night in his home office, Peter pored over Bob's documented research papers. He learned that shamanism encompasses the belief that shamans are intermediaries or messengers between the human world and the spirit world. They treat ailments and/or illness by mending the soul. Different cultures had different beliefs and different methods of healing. He read about shamans in Korea, Japan, continental Asia, Africa, southwest America, and South America.

Most were secondhand accounts. But there was the one eyewitness case Bob had told Peter about that did have a ring of authenticity. But what was that? A one-in-a-billion chance. Peter leaned back in his chair. He thought about going to bed and then in the morning calling the cancer clinic and signing on board.

Before turning off his computer, he checked his e-mail.

There was one from Bob Goodman that told him to check out an online article about shamans in Peru. Bob was a good man, a fine doctor, but sometimes he went a bit too far for Peter's pragmatic side.

But that tapping, that surge of aroused life in Peter's chest cranked up a notch. He pulled up the article by Dr. Neil M. Judd about shamans in Peru.

The Pleiades star system had a major influence on Peruvian shamans: when to sow and harvest, when the rains would arrive, and when to heal one in need. Those four words, *heal one in need,* took on a power of their own as if written expressly for Peter.

Was more at work here than the physical world? Could he, Peter Richards, a man who never bought into myth or the supernatural, possibly be in the hands of fate? There were signs, some of them only gut feelings—such as the old man not appearing in the park—others more intriguing, like Peter's inexplicable fascination with the Pleiades, and Bob steering him toward Peruvian shamans and their connection to the Pleiades.

His only option so far was to go to the cancer clinic to die and put his family through a horrible experience, much like the wife of the man in the wheelchair. He could not get that woman's worn-out face out of his mind ... especially her look of utter horror at what her life had become.

As Peter told himself to sleep on it, he heard the chime of an arriving e-mail. He checked the time on his computer. It was a quarter to two in the morning. It could be from only one person.

He opened Bob's e-mail, and in it he had written, "Before you decide anything, the archeologist who wrote the last article I sent, Neil Judd ... I want you to meet with him."

* * *

Neil Judd's home was nestled on an old country lane. Trees and foliage surrounded the house, which had a Spanish-colonial style with a low terra-cotta clay roof, stucco walls, and double-hung sash windows with carved wooden brackets and balustrades. From the driveway, a flagstone walk led to an adobe-brick courtyard with stone benches. The front door was set back by an entryway with an arched opening built of granite stones.

Peter knocked on the front door and was greeted by a gentleman in his early seventies with receding gray hair combed straight back, a high forehead, and a friendly long face. Dr. Neil Judd wore a tweed jacket with patches at the elbows and a leather string tie clipped to a white shirt by a silver clasp pitted with bits of turquoise. At first glance, this archeologist had the quiet certitude of a man of intellect who had found his calling. Here was a man who was not a stranger to himself.

"Hello, Neil Judd here. You must be Bob's friend." There was a Boston Brahmin clip to his voice, which brought to mind an Ivy League professor from an earlier time.

"Peter Richards. Thank you so much for seeing me."

"Please, join me in the sitting room." Neil offered his hand toward a raised room beyond the foyer.

Indian artifacts hung on the walls of the living room, and occupying the middle of the hardwood floor was a handwoven rug with a zigzag border in gray and black and four colorful squares in the corners, each with a half man half bird wearing a headdress. As Peter took a seat, it struck him that what he was about to hear would determine his life course from this point forward.

Peter explained his illness, the cancer clinic, and the possibility of a shaman.

"I don't know if Bob told you, but I've been traveling to Peru for the last thirty years. I work for National Geographic doing archeological research on various Indian tribes."

Peter nodded and said, "I found your article on shamans very interesting."

"Some possess very powerful medicine. There are things in this world that modern science cannot explain." Neil leaned forward in his chair, his pale eyes studying Peter to ascertain if he were a candidate for such a journey. "For years I had little regard for accounts by colleagues about the curative power of shamans. But," he said, raising a finger, "ten years ago I witnessed a crippled, arthritic man walk again."

"Oh," Peter said, leaning forward, hands on knees.

"For most of my life, Mr. Richards, I was strictly a man of science and had little credence in anything else." Neil sat back in his leather chair, his hand resting atop the end of the armrest, a carved wooden knob with the head of an eagle on its face. It was an impressive work of art. "But I have learned to keep an open mind when it comes to ancient cultures and the spirit world."

This man was no fly-by-night character. He was the real thing, a man of science who had been influenced by experiences in a far-away land. "Do you know anybody who can help me?"

"There is a village in the Andes called Abrreara."

"I heard about it in a radio interview," Peter said. "A man claimed to have been healed from a terminal illness."

"I have never been there but have heard from reliable sources that the shaman there can heal one in need."

Heal one in need. The words hung in Peter's mind much like the first time he had read Neil Judd's article. Only now, hearing them spoken by this scholarly man had a chime of validity, like hearing a bell in the belfry of an old stone church ring out the time and not questioning the accuracy.

A sense of serenity flushed over Peter, washing away his malaise like a tidal wave. "Really," Peter said as he grabbed his notepad and pen out of his jacket pocket.

Neil Judd adjusted himself in his seat and began, "You'll need a guide and transportation, and I know just the fellow ..."

On the drive home, Peter felt like his old self, his mind clear and alert, but different in that his ironclad pragmatic self had been replaced by one believing in a miracle.

He knew he was going to go to Peru to search for the shaman high in the Andes. He would contact the guide Dr. Judd had recommended, he would arrange for airfare, he would pack the necessary clothes ... The little voice in the back of his head, the one that used to control his thought process, told him to be careful, very careful. He would have to sit down with his wife and son and tell them he was going to the Andes in Peru in search of a shaman. But first he needed time to plan this thing out step-by-step.

* * *

Three days later, Peter called a family meeting at the kitchen table.

"I've decided to go to a mountain village in the Andes of Peru where there's a shaman who may be able to help me."

"Dad, a shaman in Peru, in South America?"

"Peter, a mountain village?" Debra looked at her husband as if he had lost his mind. "How in your condition are you going to do this?"

"I feel fine. I know this must sound crazy to the both of you, but what have I got to lose?"

"Peter," Debra said, "please reconsider."

"What is there to reconsider?" Peter said with a quiver of impatience. He reached for Debra's hand, but she pulled it away.

"What about us, Peter?" Debra then glanced toward Devon, who sat with his mouth open in a little circle trying to comprehend what was occurring. "Is it fair that you're running away from us?" She looked into Peter's eyes as if searching for a trace of the pragmatic man she had married and said, "When you have so little time?"

A silent pause hung in the air.

The rational side of Peter reared up. *Tell her she's right, you fool. Tell her you will go to the cancer clinic and spend your remaining time with them.* But his new spirit pushed aside his second thoughts. "I have made my decision."

"Wow." Debra let out a stream of air like an empty whistle. She glanced at a stunned Devon and back at Peter, her expression deflating from upset to hurt. "When are you leaving, Peter?" Debra's voice was thin, scarcely a thread of sound. It was a voice of surrender.

"I plan on leaving day after tomorrow."

Debra dropped her gaze emitting a low grunt. "Dear God," she said.

Devon screeched his chair back from the table, knocking it over, and stood. "It's not fair. How come Mom and I don't have a say in this?"

"No, Dev, it's not fair, but that's the way it is." Peter looked at the fallen chair and then back at his son. "So let's try and make the best of it."

* * *

The next day, Bob asked Peter to meet him at a diner near his practice for a farewell lunch.

After they ordered, Bob told Peter that Debra had come to see him at the office this morning. "She asked why I agreed with your opting to travel to Peru over treatment at the cancer clinic." They paused for a moment while the waitress brought a tea for Peter and coffee for Bob.

"You were saying."

"I told her the cold, hard fact that you have nothing to lose at this point."

"She's a good woman, Bob, even though she's upset with me."

Bob nodded in agreement. "You got that right." He put a splash of cream in his coffee and then looked out the window and then back at

Peter. "I believe some people are born in the wrong place or time in history, making them strangers to themselves." He leaned forward, his brow raised. "Do you follow?"

"Yes, I do now."

"I have a feeling, Peter, a sense, that you may be such a man, a stranger in your own world who must go out into it to find your true self." Bob took a sip of his coffee and looked back out the window. "I always thought there was a different level to you," he said, looking back at Peter, "beyond the architect and family man." He paused for a moment and then said, "Sometimes when you let your guard down at horseshoes or when you would talk about the Pleiades, I would see it in your eyes—a look, a searching."

"Six months ago, I would have said you were crazy, Bob. Now," Peter said as he lifted his cup of tea, "I could not agree with you more." He raised his tea to Bob, clinking cups.

* * *

The family's last dinner was a quiet affair. Devon and Debra hardly touched their pot roast, but Peter ate every bit. He was a man on a mission, a man with hope. He had his airline ticket, a reservation at a hotel in Lima, and the name and address of Neil Judd's guide. He had tried to reach the guide by phone but got only a recording in Spanish. He left his name and number in broken Spanish, but he never heard back.

He wouldn't think about the what-ifs. No, they were too damn scary to dwell on. He wouldn't think about all the things that could go wrong in Peru or how he had upset his family. He would think about Bob Goodman and Neil Judd, both honest, intelligent men who he was putting his faith in.

After dinner, he got his Orion refractor telescope out of the closet. "Hey, Dev, tonight's the night."

Devon was at the sink doing the dishes. "What's that?"

"The waxing gibbous moon is occulting the northern section of the Pleiades tonight. Ring a bell?"

"Oh, yeah, I forgot," he said as he placed a plate in the dishwasher.

Debra, sitting at the kitchen table, removed her glasses and looked up from the checkbook. "Dev, I'll finish up. You go on."

Devon continued to run a bristled brush in a glass filled with soapy water.

Debra came up and took the brush from his hand. "I'll take over, honey."

The boy looked up at his mother, then over to his father, and then back to his mother. "Okay, sure."

The night held wonderful potential, for the sky was clear and the moon thin. Peter assembled his telescope and tripod in the middle of the observation platform. Devon stood at the railing staring straight ahead, not up at the sky.

"Let's see if you can find the Seven Sisters, Dev."

Devon did not respond.

"Dev, I said the Seven Sisters. The Pleiades."

He looked halfway over his shoulder back at his father. "Yeah, that'd be good."

Peter made a final adjustment and stepped aside. "All right, now what's the first thing you need to do?"

Devon leaned into the eyepiece. "Follow Orion's belt up to Aldebaran." His tone was that of indifferent boredom.

"Then what?"

"I've been doing this since second grade." He adjusted the finder scope and said, "Fifteen degrees to the left and up."

"Are they shining some kind of bright blue, Dev?"

Devon drew back from the telescope. "I don't feel like it." He looked at the telescope and then at his father. "I've got homework to do."

Peter put a hand on his son's shoulder. "Please, Dev, watch the stars with me tonight."

Devon removed Peter's hand and said, "They don't interest me anymore." He opened the hatch, and down the steps and into the house he went.

Stay strong, Peter told himself. He leaned into the eyepiece and after a minor adjustment he found what he was looking for. He thought of a description by Tennyson:

Many a night I saw the Pleiads, rising thro' the mellow shade,
Glitter like a swarm of fire-flies tangled in a silver braid.

Years ago, Bob Goodman had given him a picture of the stars with the inscription, and Peter had it framed in his home office.

"Whoa, that is special," Peter said aloud. "There goes Maia into the bright side."

How he wished Devon were here to see it, but he understood where the boy was coming from. He didn't think him serious about having no interest in the stars. It was in his blood much like with Peter and Grandpa Rudy. But tonight might well have been the last opportunity with his progeny, his last chance to stargaze with Devon.

The Pleiades disappeared one by one into the light of the crescent moon. Time seemed to stop as he leaned into the lens and waited, the dark side of the moon a gray outline against the blue-black sky awash in stars.

Finally, they emerged out of the moon's dark side as if a switch had been turned on. This was an event that Peter sensed was his to observe alone as though part of a design, like a chart with his journey mapped out.

There were legends and lore about the Pleiades occultations with the moon and the planets signaling major events. Was tonight's lunar event a message to Peter?

A radio interview he had heard while having a headache had put him on this trail, an interview that the old Peter Richards would have scorned. But in his research, he investigated the connection between the shamans of the Andes and the Pleiades, a fascination of his since the first time he witnessed those glittering blue lights in the night sky. And was it just a coincidence that his primary physician suggested he look into the matter that eventually led him to Neil Judd? Were all of these coincidences?

CHAPTER 7

Peter brushed his teeth under the amber glow of the light fixture above the bathroom vanity mirror. Outside, the moody darkness pushed against the windows thwarting the light's escape.

Today was the day, the last time he might ever be in this house again. He peeked out the door and saw Debra stirring. She had tossed and turned most of the night. His wife didn't understand his going off to a remote mountain village in search of *hocus pocus*—her words. "It seems so desperate, Peter," she had told him before bed. "Where is the practical man I married?"

His family considered this journey outrageous and selfish. Outrageous, yes, but selfish, Peter thought not. He had the right to determine this course of his life's journey: it was his life.

But none of his rationalizations made it any easier. Last night when he said good night to Devon, the boy had remained his distant self. Heck, not long ago he would have thought himself mad for leaving his family like this.

He washed his mouth out and looked at himself in the mirror, standing there in his underwear. It seemed strange that anyone this healthy-looking could be terminally ill. His smooth face still had a glow of good health, the dark-brown eyes were steady and sure, the square jaw was ready for come what may, and the hair was barely flecked with gray, still with that full-bodied ripple of youth. His chest had a bit of a fleshy look as opposed to the sinewy runner's build he had from years of distance running. But still, at first glance there was a general leanness to his compact, sturdy torso.

Peter went into the closet, closed the door, and turned on the light. He put on a flannel shirt, corduroy pants, and an old pair of running shoes—he wanted to be comfortable for the long flight. When he came out, he found Debra standing in the middle of the room in her robe.

"Are you all packed?" There was a faint tremor in Debra's voice that Peter was responsible for.

"Yes, I'm good to go. Look, I know this is sudden. Not long ago, I came home to tell you and Dev I'm going to Peru, and today I'm leaving."

"Peter, what has happened to you? You've changed. First to a remote, isolated man, and now, I don't know who you are."

"Deb, I am the man you married, but a more open-minded version. There has been a chain of events that I cannot—I repeat, cannot—dismiss. Things I feel inside."

Peter gazed at her reflectively, the confident look that she had known for years. Inside, he felt calm.

"Peter, I don't understand any of this."

He took her hand in his. "I know that, Deb." He placed his free hand on her shoulder.

She sighed a nervous, jangly sigh. "Do you have your passport and cell phone?" The tremor in her voice was stronger now.

"No cell phone—it won't work where I'm going."

Debra brought a trembling hand to her mouth.

Peter wrapped his arms around her.

She placed her index and middle fingers on Peter's side, probing until she pushed against the flannel to one of the indentations, rushing his mind back to her discovery their first time together. She had told him it was like finding little secret niches that made him unique, touched by an angel.

"My God, Peter," Debra said in a choking voice as she leaned back from him. "I am afraid Devon and I will never see you again."

"Deb, I'll call you when I land in Lima." He wiped a tear streaking down her cheek and said, "From there I'll meet with the guide to see about him taking me to the shaman. After that I don't know when you'll hear from me again." He realized how hard he sounded, but he did not want to argue or try to explain that this was the right step to take. That he didn't want her to see him shrivel up and die like a drought-stricken prune. That this was the best decision all around. If he were healed, great; if he died on the way, so be it.

The *honk, honk* of a car horn broke the moment. Peter looked at her one last time. "Love you, girl." He then turned, grabbed his suitcase, and like a ghost in the night silently went down the steps.

Outside in the shadows of late night, the taxi stood out, aglow in the darkness. Peter looked over his shoulder and saw Debra at the bedroom window. He imagined how he looked, a profiled shadowy figure of a man, a stranger disappearing into the night. He raised his hand to her. She stood there for moment before turning from the window.

CHAPTER 8

Peter transferred planes in Los Angeles and Mexico City, both transfers with long delays. By the time the plane took off for Lima, it was night. Only a few passengers were on board, and Peter had the option of having an entire row to himself. But as he walked down the aisle, he neared a man in a window seat raking through a bundle of papers.

He appeared to be in his early forties, possibly forty-five, with a shock of prematurely white hair, and the air of academia about him caught Peter's attention. A little voice told him to take the aisle seat. The old Peter Richards would have dismissed that voice, but the new one didn't. Peter took the seat.

The man smiled a hello and then returned to his papers. He found a page he was looking for and began underlining.

The man, noticing Peter's interest, glanced over. "Trying to get organized."

Peter spread his hands in front of himself. "Didn't mean to be nosy."

"No, not at all," the man said as he sat back from his work. "I am preparing for a conference in Lima."

"Oh," Peter said in a tone that indicated, please, tell me more.

"Actually, I am doing research on Andean culture—mythology, to be specific." The man readjusted himself in his seat and said, "More specifically, the relationship between myth and the stars."

"Really?" Peter said as the wonder at not only the man's words but also his own decision to sit here registered in his mind.

The man studied Peter for a moment trying to determine his level of interest. "I will be speaking on a spectral star system, Algol, in—"

Peter injected, "The constellation Perseus."

"Why, yes," the man said with a trace of surprise in his voice.

Peter shrugged. "I enjoy stargazing."

"I see." The man smiled and nodded. "There is still much that isn't known about how the Incas obtained such an advanced understanding of astronomy."

"I recently read that the Incas may have invented the binary system."

"May well have," the man said. "I find them a fascinating culture, so advanced in some ways and so primitive in others."

"What do you know," Peter said, "about shamans?"

"Shamans?" The man straightened in his seat, his expression that of one finding a kindred spirit. "Well, by the way, I'm John Vander Bosch. I am on sabbatical from Stanford." He offered his hand, which Peter clasped and shook.

"Peter Richards here. Good to make your acquaintance, John. What exactly is your field?"

"Ancient cultures," John said. "I did my thesis on Inca religion and have been hooked ever since."

"I see," Peter said. A pause settled between them as he contemplated how far he should go.

John seemed to read this and said, "Do shamans interest you?"

"Yes. As a matter of fact, I am going to the Andes in search of one."

The professor leaned back, his mouth impassive, but his eyes keen with interest. "May I ask who you are looking for?"

"A shaman in the village of Abrreara."

John bit his lower lip and winced. "Is his name Concho?"

"Yes, it is."

"He passed away last week. A very unfortunate event."

"Ah … ooh." Peter grunted as he felt like a wedge had been hammered into his chest.

"Are you seeking a medical cure?"

"Yes," Peter said as he tried to quell the swell of panic at the knowledge that Neil Judd's shaman was dead. "I was diagnosed with inoperable brain cancer and was hoping the shaman could cure me."

"I am so sorry. May I ask what made you decide on this course?"

Peter told John about his headaches; nightmarish chemo treatments his college friend had received to no avail; the cancer clinic; his friend and doctor, Bob Goodman; and meeting the archeologist, Neil Judd. Then he said, "And a deep-rooted sense that I must go this route." Peter paused for a moment and said, "I can't explain it logically, it's more of a gut feeling."

John Vander Bosch placed his elbow on the armrest, leaned toward Peter, and said, "There is a village named Olaquecha," he said, shrugging as if to say this may be a long shot. "A Peruvian colleague a while back heard about an amazing incident there." He looked at Peter as if to gauge his interest.

"Please continue," Peter said.

"It is in high in the most remote part of an isolated mountain in northern Peru and was discovered less than fifty years ago." John looked up for a moment as a passenger loaded a carry-on in the overhead across the aisle from Peter. He waited until the man was seated and continued. "Occasionally, there were rumors of some miracle healing, but never was there corroboration, and as time went by, few believed them real."

Vander Bosch gave his brow a thoughtful scratch and said, "So there it stayed, a myth, until my colleague had contact with a man who claimed to have proof."

"Did he have proof?"

"Ah, yes, the sticky part. An Indian native who made his living as a mountain porter was found north of Trujillo, wandering the highway delirious and suffering from frostbite."

The flight attendant interrupted, asking Peter to bring his seat forward. He did so and said to John, "You were saying."

"He was rushed to the hospital. During his convalescence, he claimed to have been the only survivor of a group from his village who trekked the mountain seeking various cures from the shaman. My friend got wind of this and went to the hospital."

The fasten-seatbelt sign chimed on, and John clasped his on. "I know it sounds like some wild story." His attention was diverted momentarily by a late-arriving man trundling down the aisle lugging a carry-on. "But," he said to Peter, "there was physical proof. The man had been blind in one eye since childhood from a virus. There was a doctor who tended to the porter's village and verified the blindness."

The plane began to taxi, and John glanced out the window at the glitter of runway lights, before turning back to Peter. "The porter claimed his vision was restored by a shaman. They ran some tests and discovered his vision was twenty-twenty in both eyes."

"What happened to this porter?"

"This is where it gets interesting," John said, gripping the armrest as the plane picked up speed. "He disappeared from the hospital never to be seen again. One rumor is that he was heading back to Olaquecha."

Peter's old self would have laughed right in Jon Vander Bosch's face. Are you kidding me? As the plane left the ground, he leaned back in his seat trying to digest what John had told him. He heard his old pragmatic voice say, *I, for one, do not believe in myth. Turn back and spend the time left with Debra and Devon. What?* Peter thought. *Go home to die? No.* If necessary he would die in pursuit of this elusive shaman.

After the plane had picked up altitude and leveled off, Peter said, "Has anyone tried to return to this village?"

"My colleague tried, but the weather didn't cooperate … snow squalls, high winds. They abandoned the mission."

The seatbelt sign went off, and both men unclasped their belts.

The flight attendant asked if they would like a beverage. Peter passed an ice-filled plastic cup of Coke to John and took a plastic bottle of water for himself. He thanked the young woman and returned his attention to his seatmate. "Are they going back?"

John brought the middle tray down and placed his drink on it. "No, you know how these things are." He took a long swallow of his Coke and then said, "People have inspiration for a time, but then it passes and other things draw their attention." He took a sip of his drink. "After a while, it only adds credence to the myth."

Peter took a short swallow of his water and said, "Have you any interest in searching for it?"

"Me?" John laughed a deep, throaty laugh, a laugh that said, no way. "No. When I told my wife about it—she's also an anthropologist and knows full well the danger—she told me it was folly." John finished off his Coke and placed the cup on the tray. "She doesn't believe in shamanism— says it's always hearsay evidence. And she's right. I have never witnessed a shaman cure anyone, but I do know people who claim to have."

"What do you believe?"

John was silent for a moment and then said, "One very reliable man swore to me he saw a shaman levitate six inches off the ground."

"Do you believe him?"

"I believe one needs to keep an open mind."

"I don't understand why no one is pursuing the story of this shaman—"

"You said the key word, *story*," John said as he leaned back in his seat. "Few in my field believe it to be true. If you're interested, I can give you directions to the mountain."

John raised a cautionary finger. "The coup de grâce, if you will pardon my figurative expression, is that it's an arduous trek with unpredictable weather."

"I realized there were going to be obstacles on this trip." Peter folded his arms across his chest. "It is what it is. Yes, I would like directions, and if you don't you mind, John, may I pick your brain?"

John Vander Bosch nodded his approval. "Not at all, and I have a few tips about walking the Andes. First, you need a sturdy pair of boots, for where you're going is rugged terrain ..."

* * *

By the time the plane touched down at Aeropuerto Internacional Jorge Chávez, it was midmorning. Peter had slept not a wink, but he had a revved-up energy similar to that when he worked all night to meet a deadline. He and John had talked for most of the flight—or, more precisely, John had talked about a variety of subjects, from the dos and don'ts in Lima, to shamanism, to the stars—and before Peter knew it they were in a landing pattern over Lima. At the terminal, John pointed to the ATM machines along a wall. "Best bet for currency exchange."

Peter thanked him for all his help, and John wished him luck.

After getting his Peruvian sols, Peter went through customs and then got his oversized canvas suitcase on wheels from the baggage area, made his way to a line of pay phones, and called home. Debra answered.

"Hi, Deb. I'm at the airport in Lima."

"Peter," she said in a voice of relief, but with a tense pleat that seemed to stretch across a chasm that had come between them—a voice that said, You have deserted your wife and son.

"Wanted to let you know I arrived," Peter said.

"What now?"

"I am going to call the guide's office."

There was silence before Peter said, "I'll call later. Can you put Dev on?"

Another silence before, "Hi, Dad," Devon said in a brave little voice.

"I just wanted to touch base with you and your mother. I love you, Devon."

"Love you too, Dad."

Devon's voice floated in Peter's mind like gossamer silk fading away, possibly never to be heard again. *Stop it,* he told himself. *Stay steady, stay strong. No backing down now. Stay the course.*

Peter called the guide that Neil Judd had referred him to. With the help of three years of high-school Spanish and a pocket Spanish dictionary, Peter thought he understood that Aldo Coreas was expected shortly. He took out thirty sols and buried his wallet deep in his front pocket.

He started toward the exit doors rolling his bulky canvas bag on wheels behind him, when from the corner of his eye, he saw a man darting toward his flank with arm extended toward his bag.

"Taxi, señor, taxi."

John Vander Bosch had warned about touts, aggressive scammers who would want to help you find a taxi and could not be trusted. "Wave them off firmly," John had advised. "And go directly to the taxi queue and look for a compact yellow taxi. Thirty sols is your fee."

Peter stopped and turned to face his pursuer. "No, gracias," he said in a firm voice.

The man contorted his stubbly face, making a jagged scar on his cheek even more prominent and menacing. Their eyes locked, and in the man's dark, forbidding gaze there was red-streaked desperation. Peter decided to take a chance, to change things up. "Amigo," Peter said as he stepped to the side of his bag and released his hand from the handle.

A smile emerged in the corner of the man's mouth, a smile that said, I approve of your style, señor. "Sí," the man said as he led Peter out of the terminal.

Outside, the tout said, "Uno momento, señor." He left the suitcase with Peter and headed toward the taxi queue at the far end. Standing among the bustle and hustle of travelers coming and going, Peter was beginning to realize that he, Peter Richards, former stone-cold realist, was in South America—Lima, Peru, to be exact—in search of a shaman. A shaman. And he mustn't let Debra's attitude deter him. At least it seemed Devon had softened his stance.

Make every minute count, he thought as he took in the terminal, a five-story glass-façade steel structure with the control tower to its rear looming over it.

"Señor?" Peter snapped out of his architectural daydream to find the tout standing at his side. He grabbed the handle of the bag and motioned for Peter to follow over to a taxi, which reminded him of a yellow bug.

At the taxi, Peter handed five sols to the tout, who bowed his head. "Gracias, señor." He then said to the cabbie in an authoritative voice as though Peter were a man of importance, "Abrir el maletero."

The cabbie opened the trunk and loaded Peter's bag while the tout, like a poor man's bellhop, held the back door open.

After Peter was situated, the tout leaned his head into the open window, smiling an ugly yet beautiful smile. "Amigo," he said. With that, the man stepped back and walked away.

As the driver got behind the wheel, Peter leaned forward, extending a sticky note into the front seat.

"Cuánto?" Peter tapped the hotel address. "Primero." Then he tapped the guide's address. "Second."

The driver looked back at Peter and smiled, revealing a gold tooth. "Treinta más cinco."

"Bueno." Peter thought how fortunate he was to have met John Vander Bosch.

The road was not a freeway but a large divided avenue. Up a ways, they turned off onto a long street lined with colonial Spanish–style buildings painted light pink and pale blue. Farther up, they came to a wider road with an open green lined with palm trees, and in its middle was a statue of a horseman atop a massive ornate base. A few blocks up, the taxi pulled into the circular drive of Peter's hotel.

The driver removed the luggage from the trunk, and Peter said, "Uno momento." The driver smiled patiently as if he did this all the time.

After checking in and leaving his luggage at the desk, Peter found the taxi right where he had left it.

The taxi retraced its path past the open green and then turned down a side street. After puttering and weaving through a maze of narrow streets, the taxi stopped in front of a two-story limestone building, less than two miles from the hotel. The driver placed his hand atop the headrest of the front passenger seat and said over his shoulder, "Eso es todo."

Peter handed the money to the driver. "Gracias, señor."

As the taxi disappeared around a corner, Peter realized the importance of what was before him. In black raised letters on a metal plate over the front door was, "Coreas Agencia de Detectives." "Ready or not, here I am," he said aloud as he reached for the door.

After a long uncomfortable wait in a rigid chair in a cramped reception room, a man entered. He stared at his receptionist and then at Peter, like a card player considering his next move.

Peter stood. "Buenos …" He stumbled to find the words.

"Would English be better?" The man flashed a gleaming smile, accentuating his prominent cheekbones and radiant skin. His large, probing eyes, dark and heavy-lidded with a downward slant, took in the measure of Peter Richards. No more than forty, he was a handsome man of moderate size with chiseled features.

"You speak English?"

"Yes, my mother cleaned house for an American family, and I used to help her and picked it up." He shrugged as if it were no big deal. "Now, how may I help you?"

"My name is Peter Richards, and I need a guide for a mountain trek."

The dark eyes narrowed. "I am Aldo Coreas, but I am afraid you have been misinformed. I no longer do guide work."

Peter dropped his head as the lunacy of this journey began to formulate in his mind.

Aldo motioned to a door at the rear of the reception area. "My office," he said. "Let us talk."

A license of some sort hung on the wall—probably detective—of the sparse, windowless space. Coreas took a seat at a standard-issue metal desk. "Please, sit," he said, offering his hand to a folding chair situated in front of his desk.

"Why would you want to take such a journey?" Coreas glanced at his watch on his left wrist.

"I have maybe a year to live. You know of Olaquecha?"

"Olaquecha? There is mito, a myth, of a great shaman."

Peter leaned forward in his chair, fingers on his knees. "You do not believe in myth?"

"Here in the city, I do not have time for myth."

"And away from the city?"

Aldo raised his hands, a question in his eyes. "Where would one look for a myth?" he said. "Are you seeking a shaman?"

"Yes."

Aldo took in the gringo before him, scratching under his chin with his thumb and forefinger. "Where are you ill?"

Peter tapped his forehead. "Brain tumor." After a momentary pause he said, "I'm fine for now, but time is of the essence."

"You want me to take you, a man with a brain tumor, to a place high in a remote mountain"—another glance at the watch—"that may or may not have a shaman."

"Yes, that is exactly what I am asking of you," Peter said. "There is more." He proceeded to tell of meeting John Vander Bosch and his account of the shaman of Olaquecha who had healed a blind man.

"That is a good story, señor." Aldo sighed and shook his head. "Do you know how many stories like this are told in Peru? This is the land of fantasy where stories like that help those with little but dreams of better things."

Peter slid to the front of his seat and placed his hands on the edge of the desk, and he looked Aldo Coreas in the eyes. "Will you help me?"

"I am sorry, señor, but I must say no." Again, he checked the watch.

Peter noted the expensive-looking leather band and gold frame. Not the type of watch one would expect on an Andean guide. He steadied his gaze on Aldo Coreas trying to find some crack in his armor that could change this man's mind. "Do you know of anyone else who could help me?"

"There are very few men who would take such a distant journey, and they would not be available for some time."

"Can you tell me how I would go about getting there myself?"

"That is not a good idea. It is a very difficult journey. You will not make it." Aldo threw his hands up in the air. "And if by some miracle you found this village, who is to say you will find your shaman?"

"Your reasoning is all very logical, and a year ago I would have agreed with you," Peter said, meaning it. "A year ago, I would never have taken this journey." He leaned back in his chair and folded his arms across his chest. "But right here, right now, I do not have a lot of choices in this matter." He stared at Coreas for a moment and said, "Please, tell me how—"

Aldo cut in, "Are you brave or foolish or a little of both?" Again, he scratched his chin with his thumb and forefinger and looked off for a moment. Then he looked back at Peter. "My father, he die from tumor, six years today." He tapped his chest with his forefinger. "Lung." Aldo honed in on Peter. "Do you believe in destino?"

"I do now. I have to."

"As I say, six years ago today, my father, he die, and I hear his voice whisper to me, 'Ayudar a este hombre.'"

Peter made a face, trying to comprehend the words.

"Help this man," Aldo said, "is what my father told me."

Peter felt his dampened spirit rise once again. "Start tomorrow?"

CHAPTER 9

After leaving Aldo Coreas's office, Peter decided to walk back to the hotel. Actually, he did not have a choice, since there wasn't a person in sight, much less a taxi. Down a narrow street lined with four-story buildings, he stopped to admire a residence's faded mauve stucco walls with curved accolade windows in ornate black iron frames.

Farther down the street were similar designs, some with enclosed cantilevered balconies incorporated in simple masonry structures. He imagined that the balconies had come later during some period of inspiration when the buildings had too much historical significance to tear down, so a compromise was reached by installing the balconies.

The *clop, clop* of hooves on pavement drew Peter's attention. He looked over his shoulder to see a well-preserved horse-drawn carriage coming up the street with a lime-green canopy roof. The driver stopped in front of Peter. "Un paseo, señor?"

Peter started to wave him off but then stopped. "¿Cuánto?"

An easy smile spread across the young man's face. "Where?"

Peter remembered something that John Vander Bosch had told him. He bent down, tapped his shoe, and then tugged his sock. "Boots, socks."

"Ah." The driver smiled again and said, "¡No hay problema!" His expression took on a serious countenance of a young entrepreneur smelling a big pay. "Turismo?"

Peter said, "¿Cómo?"

The driver fluttered his hand in the air as if to conjure up the word. "Sightsee."

Why not? Peter thought as he said, "¿Cuánto?"

"Ciento sols."

"Okay." Peter stepped up onto a grated iron step into the backseat, which was made of black leather. He leaned forward and said, "Boots, socks, then sightsee."

"Sí." The driver raised the reins, clucked out of the side of his mouth to the horse, and off they went. They meandered through the narrow side streets passing five-hundred-year-old buildings, the tranquility broken only by the clop of hooves on the pavement.

It was hard to fathom that he was here in a horse-drawn carriage in Lima, Peru. Lima, Peru? And tomorrow he was off in search of a village high in the Andes and a shaman to find there. What if he wasn't there? *Be positive,* Peter told himself. He could do nothing about it other than see it through. And while he was at it, he would savor every moment of this adventure. Yes, Peter thought, this was his great adventure, breaking away from his old self in search of a miracle cure. And possibly, along the way, he would be searching for the missing part of himself that Bob Goodman had alluded to.

The carriage came to a stop. Up ahead was a pedestrian side street lined down the center by cast-iron lampposts. It was a lively little shopping district bulging with stucco buildings adorned with arches, porticos, galleries of arcades, and colorful flags.

The driver stepped down and swept his hands as though proudly presenting the scene. "Este calle, señor."

"Bueno," Peter said as he stepped out of the cab. He then tapped his chest. "Peter."

"Soy Edward," the driver said. He then went to a chest at the rear of the cab and removed an iron chain and lock and secured the carriage to a lamppost.

Peter and Edward spent over an hour in the shops mostly browsing, Edward keeping a careful eye on his horse and carriage.

Peter did buy an expensive but very comfortable pair of waterproof hiking boots, which Edward bartered down in price, and four pairs of waterproof socks. With the assistance of his Spanish dictionary and hand signals, Peter communicated with Edward, a short, wiry man with pale-green eyes that stood out in contrast to his dark-brown face, which held a perpetual smile. Peter thought he understood that he had inherited the horse and carriage from his uncle.

Back at the carriage Edward asked Peter, "Sightsee?"

"Plaza de Armas, Edward." In his research, Peter had learned that this was the birthplace of the government and the centerpiece of Spanish influence on art and culture. Spain had been ruthless in conquering this part of the world, destroying the ancient cultures and religions.

They parked on a residential street that faced the plaza. Edward raised his hand to indicate that he was staying with the horse and carriage.

Peter stood at the edge of the plaza, which was the width of four street blocks with a bronze fountain in the middle. In his research, he had learned that many considered it the most beautiful plaza in all of South America.

His architect's eye admired the twin-towered cathedral, the precisely placed stonework on which he stood, and the neoclassical buildings built in the late eighteenth up to the mid-nineteenth century. He walked around the perimeter of the plaza with the bright-colored buildings adorned with multiple arched balconies, tall palm trees, and well-manicured greens. Inside the cathedral he was duly impressed by the artisanship of the stonecutters who built it.

Yes, the plaza was all very fine, indeed. It could well be a city in Spain. But where was the Indian influence, that of the people from whom the Spanish had taken this land? It was as if they had never existed. The new version of himself, troubled by the lack of any trace of indigenous people, overwhelmed the architectural side in him.

Peter tipped his driver fifty sols, too much, but what the heck? Edward was a good man who surely could use the extra money. "Gracias, señor, gracias." Hand across his waist, Edward bowed in a courtly manner.

Back in his hotel room, Peter called home. After a terse "Hello, Peter," he told Debra he was leaving in the morning with his guide. "It will be the last time we talk until I return."

"Oh," Debra said.

"Deb, I need to know that you are with me on this."

Silence.

"Deb?"

"I don't have any choice at this point."

"Please, say you support me on this."

"I support you."

"Thank you," Peter said.

She asked a few questions about who the guide was, how long, and where he was going. Peter kept his answers brief and promised that he would call first thing when he returned to Lima.

Recapping his sightseeing tour, all he could get from Deb was an occasional, "Uh-huh."

After another silence, Debra said, "Here's Dev. He has some good news to share."

"Hi, Dad."

"Hey, Dev. What's the news?"

"I went to a meeting at the astronomy club at school."

"That's great," Peter said. He heard Deb in the background say something inaudible, but her tone was that of encouragement.

"Okay, M-o-o-o-m-m-m," Devon replied with gentle annoyance. "One of the kids," he said to his father, "told Mr. Brown about the platform in the backyard." The boy's voice had the same bruised vulnerability, but with it an uptick of anticipation as if the stargazer in him were reawakening. "Mr. Brown—he runs the club—asked if we could meet sometime in the backyard to stargaze." There was a question in Devon's voice. Peter couldn't tell if he was asking permission or weighing whether he wanted to do it.

"Why don't you make it a campout in the backyard?"

"Yeah?"

"Sure, then we'll both be sleeping under the stars, but I'll be in the Southern Hemisphere."

After Peter gave a brief recap of his time in Peru, he said, "I love you, Dev."

"Love you too, Dad."

Debra came back on, and he told her it was important that the only two people that mattered to him were behind him on this. "Please, Deb. Devon seems to be coming around. I need your blessing on this."

"I can say whatever you like, Peter, but I won't mean it."

"Tell me you love me."

"Peter?"

"Yes, Deb."

"Please be careful."

"I will."

"And call the moment you return."

"Tell me you love me, Deb."

"I will always love you, Peter."

Peter went to the window. Night had fallen over the city, stars glimmering high in a blue-black Peruvian sky. Those sparkling images from long ago may help Devon get over a rough patch. And he seemed to be handling Peter's trip better than Deb. He wished she were behind him on this journey, but when she said, "I will always love you, Peter," the tenor of her voice left no doubt. It had a soothing effect on Peter to hear those words from her. But he couldn't fool himself—this journey gnawed at her. He wondered how well Deb thought she knew her husband.

For that matter, he didn't know quite who he was anymore. The metamorphosis he was going through, all while fighting a terminal illness, had given him a sense that he had never been truly familiar with himself. He remembered Bob Goodman's words at the diner. "Some people are born in the wrong place or time in history, and that makes them strangers to themselves." Bob had leaned forward, his brow raised. "Do you follow?"

Yes, he did follow. What would have seemed preposterous had growing traction. Peter Richards, the one he had created, had played a role like a character in a story. This emerging person was on a journey to find his true self—whoever that might be.

He turned from the window and to his bed.

Lying under the covers, he whispered, "Stay steady. Stay strong."

Peter woke before dawn. He had slept reasonably well, the bed firm but comfortable. His sleeping quarters for the near future would be firm, but comfortable? *A small price to pay,* he thought as he went to the window.

There wasn't a soul about the city. Streetlamps illuminated the Plaza de Armas in an eerie shade, tempering the bright colors of the city in a muted glow. Yellow light came from the belfries of the twin towers of the cathedral, standing out like beacons against the dark silhouette of hills in the distance. Today was the first day of the rest of Peter Richards's life—a new life.

After showering, Peter emptied his suitcase on the bed, including a backpack he had purchased when he and Debra took their first canoe trip together. It was worn and ragged in spots but still had everything he needed, with plenty of straps and compartments, suspension mesh at the bottom for additional items, and a metal external frame that distributed the weight of the load. They had crammed it with clothes and canned goods, and then tied a tent on top and a sleeping bag on the bottom. She had carried a smaller backpack with leftovers.

The trip was a seminal moment in their relationship. Not only did they make love for the first time, but the outdoor experience with Debra confirmed that this girl was the one.

She had no experience canoeing or camping but was a trouper the entire time, never once complaining. Also, Peter learned that she possessed a sharp wit. Debra had noticed an identification tag on the pack, "Jasper No. 4374." "We proclaim that this backpack is designated The Jasper." She tapped a stick on the pack like a queen knighting a soldier and said, "And for the rest of our days we shall search this land far and wide for the 4,373 missing Jaspers." That first trip became known as The Jasper.

The plan was that once they were married, Debra would continue teaching grade school for a few years and then they would begin a family. When Peter wanted to leave a well-paying job and start the business with Tim and Bill, Debra had been all for it. Devon was an infant at the time, and she volunteered to return to work if money became an issue. "You're a fine architect, Peter, and deserve this opportunity. I know you will succeed."

That was Debra, offering to do whatever was necessary for the good of the family. And with this old, beaten-up backpack, a part of her was with Peter here in Peru. And so was Devon, for they had used the pack on many a campout, stargazing with binoculars much like Peter had with Grandpa Rudy.

Peter stowed all four new pairs of socks in the bottom of the main compartment. Nine-year-old Devon had told him on preparing for their second camping trip, to observe a lunar eclipse, that he wanted extra socks. "I can take anything, Dad, but dirty, wet socks." Peter had tried to explain that they could wash the socks in the creek and then dry them by the campfire. The boy scrunched up his face. "Yuck." He then said in an emphatic voice of someone much older, "No, Dad. I want fresh, clean socks."

Peter remembered laughing, a tilt-back-your-head laugh that shook his shoulders. He tousled Devon's hair. "Clean and fresh socks it is, my good man." Ever since, Peter had packed extra socks, and this trip would be no different.

Besides the socks, Peter packed two long-sleeved T-shirts, four pairs of underwear, two pair of hiking pants with extra pockets, two tightly knitted, lightweight cotton sweater-shirts, a windbreaker, and his new hiking boots. The rest of his clothes he stuffed in his suitcase, which he would leave in Aldo's car. He had enough room for dry goods, utensils, and such that Aldo was bringing. Leery of drinking any of the local water, Peter filled his canteen with bottled water and packed iodine drops for when his supply ran out.

At dawn, Peter found Aldo standing next to a heavy-duty SUV in the hotel's circular drive.

They drove around the Plaza de Araya, through the narrow streets lined with colonial-style buildings, and onto the divided avenue. Past the city limits, box houses popped up on a hillside. It seemed a place trapped between the glamorous city and the rugged terrain in the distance, a place unsure of its identity. Back home these ramshackle places would be considered poverty level, but here Peter wondered if they weren't considered middle class.

They turned onto a highway, the Pacific Ocean on their left and nothing but open space and mountains ahead. Aldo said, "We drive north past Trujillo and will spend the night at posada. Nine, maybe ten hours we drive today. Mañana, we drive east toward the mountains, where we stay below for a while."

"Stay below?"

"The base of the mountain is higher than Lima, but where we go is very high. We must get some altitude in your blood before we climb the mountain."

The conversation was kept to a minimum, as Aldo seemed to sense that Peter would appreciate some quiet time. He was in a subdued state of garnering his inner self for the strength needed for what lay ahead.

A couple of hours into the journey, they drove along a desertlike coastline. Aldo lifted his index finger off the steering wheel. "There, the Andes."

Up ahead a pale-blue outline of mountains loomed over the horizon. The sight of it held Peter for a moment. Somewhere high up there, he hoped, was a man from whom he would seek his salvation.

They stopped twice in rural villages for gas, but both were out. Aldo told Peter not to worry, for he had two five-gallon cans of gas in the back. "We will find gasolina." The third stop was a desolate little village off the highway. There was an adobe building with a gasoline pump in the front. Next to the front door was a wooden placard with "Comida" scrawled in bright red.

Aldo went inside and came back out with an old man in a flannel shirt, knee-length trousers, and sandals. His thick mop of black hair, without a trace of gray, was parted down the middle in stark contrast to his craggy brown face, which had a look of tuckered-out weariness. He gestured for Aldo to fill the car and turned to go back in when he looked over at Peter inside the car. He squinted hard for a moment. In those small, dark eyes was a question—Something out of the ordinary brings you here, no? Then he made his way back inside the store.

Peter got out of the car. If this place had a name, he saw no sign or indication. Farther up the rutted dirt street were a smattering of disheveled shedlike living quarters where two barefoot boys kicked a matted ball made of some type of fibrous plant or grass.

There was an emptiness about this little nothing place, littered with five-gallon buckets and rusted shells of compact cars. Even with the scalloped russet hills rising up to meet a crystal-blue sky, this place could not be called anything but defeated. These people were far from the city in this mountainous land, but it came upon Peter that they did not live in the mountains—they existed.

The old man came back out of the store with a tray of two bowls of some sort of stew and a stack of flatbread. He placed it on a wooden table with four rickety-looking rattan chairs. Aldo paid the man and said, "Gracias, señor." The old man stole another glance at Peter and then went back inside.

The warm and spicy stew contained bits of potatoes, corn, and some colorful root vegetables that Peter wasn't familiar with. He was curious about the stew, the old man, and what these people were doing in the middle of nowhere, but he didn't inquire. Much as he considered these people as existing and not living, he felt similar in this transitional state from his old life to his destination—an in-between man. And until the journey began, which in his mind was the hike or at least the end of traveling by car, he would watch and listen.

Past Trujillo, Peter said, "Aldo, I don't mean to be so quiet."

Aldo turned to Peter. "Silence will be our companion on our journey."

CHAPTER 10

The adobe posada was situated on the side of a hill, overlooking the ocean, now shimmering in the afternoon light. The one-story rectangular building, with rounded corners, was a faded eggshell color and appeared sturdy if roughly built with a coarse finish on the walls. There was a serenity to this ordinary-looking posada, backdropped by a smattering of small trees, as though it had shrugged itself out of the side of the hill.

While Aldo checked in, Peter stood at the top of a set of timber-and-earthen steps carved into a scrubby hillside down to the shoreline.

Out in the sea, a native, wearing only a loincloth, paddled a dugout canoe north beyond the break. Even from afar, there was something primitive yet compelling about this lone individual. His strokes seemed effortless, two on one side and then the other. Peter wondered where he was going and what his life was like. No doubt it was difficult, each day struggling against the elements, or had this man found his solace in this simple, rugged existence?

Returning to the posada, Peter met Aldo waiting at the front entrance.

"Get some rest, and I will meet you out here after."

Peter's room had no door and was minimal, with a single bed, a washstand with a basin, and a picture of Jesus on the wall. A communal toilet was at the end of the hall.

He was stripping away not only the layers of his inner self but also his outer world to a new reality on the horizon—a silent world, different yet comforting.

After a nap, Peter went back outside, where he found Aldo striding up the hillside steps clutching a string of fish.

"We eat good meal," Aldo said as he reached the top. "I have pescado."

"They look like ocean flounder," Peter said. "How did you catch them?"

Aldo tapped a backpack on his back. "Retráctil fishing rod."

"I see you are prepared."

Aldo slipped out of his backpack. "I clean fish, then we make fire." He nodded as if agreeing with himself and looked at Peter. "Can you find stones and wood?"

"Okay," Peter said with a question in his voice.

Aldo shifted his attention to the hillside and said, "Stones there." He took a burlap sack from the backpack and handed it to Peter. He then settled his gaze on a patch of scrub trees. "Look for any branches on the ground, but do not disturb the trees." Aldo raised his index finger as if to say one more thing. "Also, collect any brush or dead grass."

"All right," Peter said. "I'll meet you back here."

At the top of the hillside, Peter scanned the rocky incline—not too steep. He sidestepped his way down the slope, carefully avoiding the needles of spiny scrub plants and boulders wedged into the sandy soil, to collect stones the size of a fist.

He slung the sack of stones over his shoulder, steadied himself, and climbed three steps and then a landing, three steps and then a landing, his way up the hill. He returned to Aldo, who had already skewered two fish.

Peter emptied the sack of stones. "They good?"

Aldo glanced at the stones and returned to cleaning the last fish with a pocketknife. "Bueno."

"I'll get the wood."

The patch of gnarly, twisted trees reminded Peter of mesquite. They bore spines with yellow flowers, and long greenish-yellow pods resembling peas. He opened a pod to discover small brown seeds. He placed the tip of his tongue on a seed. It was surprisingly sweet with a wild honey-sugary taste.

Peter put his hand on a tree trunk. This was hard wood, wood that he imagined had endured many years in this gritty, sandy soil.

Tufts of parched long grass, twigs, and a smattering of branches covered the ground. The grass came up with little resistance. He stuffed it into the sack along with the other debris.

"You don't waste any time," Peter said as he found Aldo placing the last of the stones around a six-inch-deep pit.

Aldo nodded and motioned for the sack.

"Not much," Peter said as he handed the sack to Aldo, who emptied the contents on the ground.

"No, the Huarango is a strong, greedy tree that can live a thousand years." He gathered the dead grass, rolled it into a ball, and showed it to Peter—exhibit one. "It doesn't even allow the grass to survive." Aldo crouched down on his haunches and put the ball of grass in the center of the pit.

Peter sat, crossing his legs in front of himself. "This seems an arid climate—probably not much rain."

They exchanged a quick glance, and Aldo nodded—please continue.

"I bet the tree roots leave little moisture for anything else trying to grow."

"Bueno, Pedro. It is so." Aldo looked toward the trees. "The grass starts to grow when there is lluvia." He raised his hands over his head and lowered them, flicking his fingers. "But, no lluvia, the Huarango takes all the water from the earth. It once covered much terrain, the Huarango, but the people cut it down for firewood and charcoal." Aldo smiled a thin, ironic smile. "Its one enemy is more greedy."

Aldo built a tepee of kindling from the twigs and then stacked branches around them. He lit the ball of dry grass with a match. "Now we wait."

The guide's expression revealed nothing. Yesterday in his office, he had seemed like any businessman in a big city, constantly checking his watch ... the squinting of his eyes when Peter had asked him to guide, the quick shake of the head. But in this land of mountain and sky, he was a different hombre, the shrewd gleam in the eyes replaced by the glint of a man on an adventure. It seemed a mask had been removed and in its place emerged a man of the earth, la tierra.

When red-hot coals remained, Aldo handed a skewered fish to Peter, keeping two for himself. "Hold the fish over like this, Pedro." Aldo held his fish an inch over the coals, rotating every so often. When they were done, they removed the skewers and placed their catch on tin plates.

Peter took a chunk of fish off his plate and jiggled the hot meat in his hands. It had a sweet, succulent flavor. "It is very good."

Aldo offered a smile mostly to himself. "Tomorrow we drive three hours, maybe four, before we come to the foot of the mountain." He tore off a section of fish and handed it to Peter.

Peter said, "How long a hike to Olaquecha?"

Aldo looked at Peter, kindly appraising his client. "If the weather is bueno, maybe three days, maybe more. Time can stand still in these mountains."

Peter raised his chin in the direction of Aldo's bare wrist. "No use of a watch then?"

Aldo leaned his head forward and raised his eyebrows in a silent touché. "You see things, Pedro, that others, perhaps, may miss." He dug into his backpack and removed a digital watch similar in appearance to those worn by many of Peter's fellow runners.

"Compass watch, amigo," Aldo said as he secured it on his wrist. "Different land, different watch."

After the meal, Aldo retired to his room. Though tired, Peter decided that he needed some time to ponder things.

On the way down the steps to the ocean, he considered Aldo's expression when asked how long to the mountaintop. His guide's gaze bespoke tact and understanding toward a man with little time left on this earth. This was an act of kindness, a good deed, toward a man with a terminal illness, a favor to his father's ghost. Get the gringo up the mountain to show him there is no village, no shaman, and then guide him down the mountain so he may go back to his country to die.

The red sun, tilting on the horizon, emitted shafts of golden-orange light splaying out across the water. Waves broke gently on the shore. Peter stood on a long stretch of beach, to his right a stone jetty, the only trace of human influence. A breeze rolled over the water caressing his face. Far from home, Peter Richards had tapped into a dormant, unknown part of his subconscious. An adventurous, go-for-broke, question-all-that-you-had-ever-believed individual was now taking form on his journey for a miracle.

Beyond the break, he saw a small figure in a canoe, the same nomad from before. The man was hurling a spear into the choppy water, and after three attempts it came up with a fish, twice the size of any of Aldo's catch. He reached for his paddle, stopped as people do when sensing they are being watched, and looked toward the shoreline. He paused for a second; his brown body appeared so small and insignificant in the ocean. He then raised his right hand toward Peter.

Peter returned the gesture. He held his hand out until the man paddled out of sight around a jut of land.

* * *

At dawn, they departed the posada. After a while, hardly a car or truck did they see.

"Soon we will gain altitude, Pedro," Aldo said as they passed a cluster of adobe structures at the end of a dirt road off the highway. He told Peter they were on the Central Highway that ran the length of Peru. "Panamericana Norte, numero uno."

"Uh-huh," Peter replied as he took in the barren beauty. The green-blue ocean below stretched out to the pale horizon, and to their right, behind the village, ocher-colored hills slanted upward until land met sky.

An hour past the rural village there was no trace of civilization. Ahead, the snowcapped Andes dominated the landscape like giant sentries.

They turned off the highway, rattling along a valley floor, the mountains closing in on them.

Farther up, Aldo slowed down as they banged and bumped along over the rocky, rutty ground. They drove parallel to a stream speckled with boulders and stones bordering its shoreline. Nearby, sheep grazed in a field of wild grass, past which was a stretch of undulating terrain ending at the base of a mountain shrouded in mist. What a sight. What a mountain.

It matched John Vander Bosch's description of a stream and foothills at the mountain's base. *Here it is,* Peter thought. A surge of energy like an electrical current of joy ran through him. *Yes, this is it.* He and Aldo were at the start of a new journey, a new beginning. Never had he seen a more exhilarating sight than this rugged, ancient mass of stone.

"Look to your right, Pedro." Aldo tipped his head toward an adobe hut with a thatched roof and a hide flap doorway. "It appears that providencia is with us," he said as he brought the car to a stop.

A man, an Indian, with a face as weathered and craggy as the mountains, came out of the hut wearing a red poncho with a high rolled collar, knee-length trousers, and leather sandals. He was short legged but with a long, stout torso that gave the impression of strength.

Aldo spoke to the man in a strange tongue with power and conviction as though the language excited him.

The man replied in a breathy, guttural burst of words with a singsongy harmonic quality that drew Peter's ear.

He motioned for Aldo and Peter to come inside his hut.

On one side was a layer of straw with an animal hide for a blanket. A few steps across the dirt floor were three wicker storage bins. It was a cramped, stark space.

"Peter, this is Havo. He has been grazing his sheep. This is his outpost." Aldo put his hand on Peter's shoulder and said, "Pedro."

"Hmm." In Havo's gaze there seemed an intuitive knowledge that understood Peter thoroughly.

"I will ask if he knows the way up the mountain to Olaquecha."

Havo listened intently and then responded. His words had the tonal qualities of a rehearsed speech.

"He says he has no knowledge of Olaquecha. He says the mountain is vacant. No one lives in the mountain."

"Tell him why I am here, Aldo."

"Whatever he knows, his loyalty will not be to us."

The old man looked at Peter, a mysterious tranquility in his dark eyes.

"Tell him, Aldo," Peter demanded.

Aldo put emphasis on certain words, no doubt telling Havo not only about Peter's illness but also the story of the lost porter who claimed to have been healed by a shaman from this mountain.

When Aldo finished, the old man stood stoically staring at Aldo and then at Peter. After more contemplation, he spoke to Aldo.

"He says, Pedro, he welcomes our stay with him."

Havo appeared to be in his seventies, but those eyes, which slanted down at the corners, looked like they had seen many more years pass with a ken beyond the scope of the here and now. Old Havo looked to have been hatched out of the side of the great mountain.

Peter leaned his head toward Aldo but remained looking at Havo. "Tell him the mountain's secrets are safe with us. That I only seek the shaman."

Aldo started to speak, but Havo raised his hand, his eyes fixed on Peter. "Quy nuqa timpu."

And then Peter saw it—conflict in his eyes.

Aldo said, "Give him time."

"Fair enough." Peter bowed slightly toward Havo and then said to Aldo, "What is the language you two speak?"

"It is Quechua, the Indian tongue—when an Indian gets near his tierra natal," Aldo said in a wistful voice. "My father's side is Spanish, but my mother's Indian. So," he said, tapping his chest with his fist, "I feel the call of the mountain. My blood is called Mestizo." Aldo put his hand on Havo's shoulder. "Quechua." He strung out the word with emphasis on the final consonant so it came out *ketch chew* Wa.

Havo uttered a concurring grunt and then spoke to Aldo.

"He is going to make a fire," Aldo said.

Havo removed a cylindrical-shaped mesh sack from one of the wicker baskets and went outside. He walked with an easy gait; everything about him said, no hurry. Wandering through his sheep, he collected droppings of dung, placing them in the bag.

Aldo and Peter stood outside the hut. "What's he doing, Aldo?"

"Here, in this land," Aldo said, stretching his arms out to his sides, "one must waste nothing." He looked over toward the stream. "Let us gather stones for the fire."

Havo patiently kindled the dung fire with a golden disk off the rays of the late-day sun. A blue smokeless flame emerged from a bed of dry grass under the dung. He blew gently on the flame until the fire was secure. He then placed a good-sized flat stone over the fire. From a blue-and-red-checkered mesh sack, he emptied a generous portion of bite-sized potatoes that he then loaded on wooden skewers. He laid the skewers on top of the flat stone, turning them every so often. They sat in silence waiting for the potatoes to cook, an easy comforting silence as though they were all old acquaintances.

When the potatoes were done, Aldo handed tin plates to Havo and Peter. Then from his backpack he took out a roll of stringy dried beef. He unpeeled a portion and handed it to Havo. "Aycha." He handed Peter some. "Carne, Pedro."

After the meal, as the last glimmers of sunlight dipped behind the mountains, the warmth of the day went with it. Havo stood and spoke briefly to Aldo.

"Havo is going to sleep with his sheep tonight and wants you to take his bed."

"No," Peter said, raising his hand in protest.

"Yah," Havo said, nodding.

Peter looked at Aldo. "Where will you sleep?"

"I will dream under the stars, amigo … under the stars."

* * *

A dawn-gray sky greeted Peter as he emerged from the hut. Aldo sat cross-legged at a fire warming a couple of skewers of potatoes. The sheep and Havo were gone. It seemed to Peter as though the old shepherd had tapped into a unique vitality from this land, a land that had begun to take hold of Peter. Not only its quiet, eerie beauty but the pristine, rugged environment had settled him down from the jangled ball of nerves he had been of late, and he'd not had a headache since he arrived.

Aldo looked up as Peter approached. "How did you sleep, Pedro?"

"Good—real good."

"This land can do that if one will listen to its whispers."

Peter noted the red poncho at Aldo's far side. "Where is Havo?"

"He will return," Aldo said as he turned the skewers on the flat stone over the coals. "He left you this." Aldo leaned his head toward the poncho.

Peter stepped around his guide and picked it up. He ran his hand down the solid-red material; how soft and yet strong it felt. He raised it over his head and put it on. The rolled collar nestled onto the sides of his neck as if designed for him.

Aldo grinned and said, "Now you look like a man of these mountains."

Peter sat down with legs crossed and said, "Why did he leave me this?"

Aldo handed Peter a skewer of the potatoes on a plate. "He did not say." He stripped his potatoes with a pocketknife onto his plate and said, "It is unusual with no patterns other than this." Aldo tugged the waistband, which was checkered with black and white squares. He gave out a look with raised eyebrows that suggested this poncho was something special. "And," he said, "I have never seen one with such a collar." Aldo shrugged and looked off before returning his gaze to the fire. "Today we begin your regimen, to get the altitude in your lungs."

"Regimen? What's the plan?"

Aldo held a potato between his thumb and forefinger, blowing on it. "We will walk with full packs to get ourselves ready." Aldo plopped the potato in his mouth, swelling his cheek. He made a casual gesture with his hand toward the mountain and said, "To climb that giant."

After they ate, they went to the rear of the SUV. Aldo raised the back door, stuck his head in, tapped Peter's backpack, and said, "I have better pack for you."

"No," Peter said, shaking his head, "I am going to use this. It works for me."

"Pedro, I have lighter, better pack that will make journey easier for you." Aldo reached in and removed a sleek-looking nylon backpack. "Tell you what. We pack what we will carry up the mountain on our exercise today. I promise you will see a difference."

Peter feared he would lose a connection to Debra and Devon by not taking his old pack. Yeah, yeah, he knew he was in some form of transition, but this was too abrupt. "Aldo—"

"Look at me, Pedro."

Peter turned to face his guide.

"You must trust me, amigo." Aldo handed the backpack to Peter. "We are going to travel ligero, little weight."

"It is light," Peter said.

"Sí," Aldo said as he made a face that said, told you so. "We use extralight bedrolls, no tent. We will find our shelter."

Aldo fumbled around and brought out two nylon bedrolls. He unrolled one and zipped it open to reveal a tightly stitched fleece liner. "Warm but less than half a kilo. We will face many challenges." He picked up Peter's old backpack. "We do not require any more than what the mountain will provide." He placed Peter's backpack down. "I am sure there are many memories with this." Aldo jerked his thumb sideways toward the looming mountain. "But there is no room for sentiment where we go."

Aldo loaded the packs, with his carrying all of the food supplies of dried-meat strips wrapped in tinfoil, flatbread, potatoes, and plastic bags of grain. Peter asked to carry more than his clothes and a full canteen, but Aldo waved him off.

"From here until we get there." Aldo tipped his head in the direction of the mountain. "I am el jefe, the boss, Pedro."

They walked along the stream until they came to the foothills. "These estribaciones will be a good start," Aldo said. They were low-slung at the base but quickly rose into steep, choppy slopes of rust-colored hard earth. Behind the foothills were larger hills splintered into a diversity of hues from shadow to sunlight.

It seemed a forgotten place untouched by civilization, with a vigor that had endured through the ages, an unconquerable spirit that had escaped the grip of humanity. In this land of mountains and sky, a spark of a notion coalesced that this journey was meant to be, had to be.

They walked in silence. Aldo led, occasionally looking back, waiting, and then pushing on as they maneuvered their way up and down, and around and over ridges, fissures in the land, steeps, and inclined screes littered with loose rock. Peter's main concern was not to catch his foot in crevices of the uneven terrain.

By the time they stopped to eat, Peter was winded. They ate flatbread and meat strips on the side of a foothill. "How is the backpack, Pedro?"

"You were right. It is good, very good."

Aldo inclined his head as if to say, I told you so. "From here we head back. Mañana we do more, next day more still, and then we see."

For three days, they walked the foothills. Each day Aldo pushed them further. And each day Peter gained endurance, his years of distance running paying off, though he was sore in his thighs and shoulders. The new boots were light and durable, but his feet were adjusting to them, resulting in blisters on his toes, a small inconvenience in comparison to what lay ahead. Peter intentionally avoided looking at the looming mountain, which dominated this land like a forbidding megalith.

After the third day of hiking, Aldo led Peter to the back of his SUV. "We pack for departure in morning."

"What about Havo?" Peter said. "I thought we were waiting to hear back from him about the best way up the mountain."

"You do not hear that?"

Peter squinted at Aldo, not sure what he meant. Then he heard the faint bleating of sheep.

Aldo looked over his shoulder toward the stream, where the sheep were drinking along the water's edge. Havo raised a walking stick in greeting.

* * *

The dung fire had died down to glowing embers. Their food had been eaten in silence. Never had Peter lived in such silence. It seemed as much a part of this world as blue sky and mountains.

Havo brought his feet up in a cross-legged squat, locking his arms around his knees with hand clasping wrist. "Qusmi Runa," he said as he raised his chin in the direction of the mountain.

Peter turned to his guide, who kept his gaze on Havo.

"Cloud People," Aldo said, raising a finger for patience.

Havo spoke in his singsongy way, raising and lowering his voice with the cadence of one telling a story. In the old man's eyes there was a glimmer of reminiscence, reminding Peter of his grandfather Rudy telling stories of his boyhood.

Aldo said, "There is a group of people who live high in the mountain, people who seek only to live among themselves. They live in the mist and clouds and are known as the Cloud People, Qusmi Runa."

"Yah," Havo grunted in confirmation.

Peter was anxious to ask about the shaman, but instead he offered his hand for Havo to continue.

The storyteller tone left Havo's voice, as he seemed to be giving Aldo directions. His head tilted left or right, the chin rising and lowering as he spoke in a controlled cadence to Aldo, who interjected for clarifications.

When the old man finished, he crossed his hands on his chest and nodded his head—that is all.

"To find this village, one must look for signs along the way." Aldo poked the embers in the fire with a stick and said, "He left Olaquecha many years ago but says his memory of the route is strong."

"What about the shaman, Aldo? The shaman."

"No." Havo said. He spoke to Aldo in a short burst and then looked hard at Peter.

"He will not speak of the shaman," Aldo said. "But he offers the path up the mountain on your Raru purly apu." The guide and the old man exchanged knowing glances, and then Aldo said to Peter, "On your spirit journey."

Peter raised his tin toward the wanderer and spat out, "Agra dis i koo key."

The wanderer tilted his head toward Peter. "Imamanta."

After they ate, Aldo spoke to Yachay, and Peter heard, "Olaquecha."

The wanderer remained silent for a moment. "Yah," he grunted.

Aldo said, "Shaman chaypi?"

Peter leaned forward, waiting for Yachay's response. The wanderer took a deep inhalation. Finally, he exhaled and nodded yes.

"Does the shaman live in the village, Aldo?"

"Sí, Pedro."

"Yes," Peter said with a rise of emotion in his voice. "Yes."

Aldo then asked Yachay if he was bothered by the village or the shaman.

Yachay shrugged nonchalantly and then told Aldo that he had trouble living in a village, any village.

Aldo asked Yachay what the shaman was like.

"Hatun kallpa."

Aldo asked if there was something about the shaman that Yachay did not like.

The Indian sat stone-faced staring at Aldo. "Hatun kallpa."

Aldo brought his hands up and tipped his head toward Yachay to indicate he was done and thank you. "He has not been to the village for some time, but the shaman is there."

"What else, Aldo? Something did not seem right."

Aldo said, "Hatun kallpa, the shaman has great power."

"Yah, nisiu," Yachay said.

"He says the shaman has too much power for his liking."

"How so, Aldo?"

Yachay was listening.

Aldo said to Yachay, "Vagabundo qispi."

Yachay furrowed his brow and nodded in agreement.

"He must be free. He cannot live in structure." Aldo opened his hands toward the wanderer and said in a raised voice, "Yachay qisqi.'

Yachay grinned and said, "Chiqaq." *True.* He raised his chin to Peter and said, "Nowask'a mana risisqa." He tapped his chest with his fist. "Wawqi."

Aldo said, "You are no longer mana risisqa—stranger—to Yachay, but a wawqi, friend."

Yachay tapped his chest again. "Yah, wawqi."

Peter tapped his chest and said, "Yachay, wawqi."

The wanderer's eyes shined at Peter. He was enjoying the company, and Peter wondered if two guests were his limit. He then spoke in a rapid burst to Aldo, stopped for a moment, and then spoke some more.

"He says that when the god Viracocha is at your side, the mountains and sky are your friends." Aldo poked the dying fire with a stick, shooting little red sparks that quickly died in the fading light. "But when one crosses Viracocha, bad things will befall him."

Yachay spoke again.

"When you arrive at your destination," Aldo said, "you must be careful of who and what to believe. You must listen to your heart, your sunqu, and your mind—"

Yachay cut in, his voice more measured. "Sunqu chuchu pis mosphon allin, kuphiiyay paykuna."

"He says your heart is strong and your mind is good. Trust them." Aldo squinted a look at Peter that said, You have come far, but there is still more, much more to go.

CHAPTER 12

Half-asleep, Peter sensed the darkness abating. He had awoken in the middle of the night not able to see his hand in front of his face. Or was that a dream? He wasn't sure. But in that darkest of dark, he sensed a presence, a force that was with him on this journey.

As the sleep faded, his conscious mind began to wake, while something faintly familiar stirred. Was it the warmth of the poncho and his bedroll? Or the faint light seeping into the hut like an old friend visiting from long ago? Something innate told him not to overthink it but to let it come.

The soft tremor of a flute whispered in his ear. Yachay must be playing, but it seemed far away.

Outside his hut, Peter spotted Aldo down below sitting cross-legged warming two spits of potatoes over a fire. These mountains had washed away his worldly air, revealing a stoic countenance, no doubt from Indian blood that coursed through his veins.

At the fire, Peter asked, "Where is Yachay?"

Aldo handed Peter a plate of potatoes. "He go."

"He left?"

Aldo looked off for a moment and then back at Peter. "He is a vagabundo, a wanderer. He cannot stay in one place too long."

Peter stripped the potatoes onto his plate. "Did Yachay say how far to the village?"

"Two more days." Aldo rolled a strip of meat in a ball and bit into it. "This is much different than where you come from, no?"

"Yes, much different," Peter said as he took a bite of his meat, followed with a potato, and he gasped at its heat.

"What do your wife and son think of you coming here?"

"Both are concerned, especially my wife. She thinks I've gone off the deep end." Peter twirled a hot potato in his fingers. "She is a good woman but does not understand why I left her and my son." Peter raised a hand to indicate, enough. "Tell me about you, Aldo. Any family?"

"I have a son," Aldo said with a lift in his voice. "When he was born, I made a promise that I would always be there for him and love him. Oh, such a beautiful niño ..." He looked at Peter and smiled a crooked, bittersweet smile. "He lives in Montevideo, in Uruguay, with his mother." Aldo gave his head a little shake. "It is complicated. His mother, from a rich and powerful family, was a client. I was following her husband, a wealthy businessman who was in Lima on business, and found him unfaithful. We fell in love ... or I did anyway. I haven't seen my son in four years." A look came over his eyes, eyes that seemed to say, if only. "She divorced her husband and remarried, and they won't allow me access to my son. Now I am a stranger to my own hijo."

They exchanged a glance, and then Aldo said, "That is life, unpredictable. We must take what it gives us and go on." He took a sip of water from his canteen and said, "For one never knows how the story will end." Aldo laughed a short, ironic laugh. "I ask about your family and tell you my problems."

Aldo looked over his shoulder, holding his gaze on the trail for a beat, and then back at Peter. His expression had returned to that of trail guide. "We climb higher still today. Let us eat and be on our way." He stripped the potatoes off his skewer and began eating in earnest.

Past the bend where they first saw Yachay descending the mountain, and then up a steep, windy incline, they came to a fork in the road. Aldo looked to his right. "Yachay's shortcut."

Peter squinted up at the steep path bordered with boulders. Off in the pale-blue distance, a line of mountains, with crests of glittering snow, rose into the infinite Andean sky. It seemed a timeless, vast place, so strange and daunting and—dare he say it—alluring. Yes, alluring, as though some ghostly mountain entity were encouraging him on. Climb higher, hombre, climb higher, for there is more for you to see and learn.

"I am starting to understand," Peter said, "how all of this can take a hold of a person like Yachay."

"The shaman is alive and lives in the village."

"Yes," Peter said as he short-jabbed his fist in the air.

Aldo spoke again to the boy, who had a look of confidence—not cocky, just that it seemed he knew who he was and where he was going in this life.

"Pedro, he asks us to join him for chicha."

"What is his name?"

"He has not said. But he says we are welcome to spend the night." Aldo smiled at the boy as though he were an old acquaintance. He said to Peter, "Also, he says that if we leave early mañana, we will make it to village in a day and a half."

The boy tilted his head toward the hillside.

"Come, Pedro, chicha awaits us."

The boy's living quarters were twice the size of Havo's cramped one-man hut. In the middle of the space, Peter and Aldo sat at a crude table made of logs roughly mortised and tenoned together. Their chairs were made of wood and vines, the floor was hard-packed earth, and the dirt walls were braced by wood planks. On one side of the space were two woven mats made of reeds and grass, each with a blanket rolled up at the head; and on the other side there were three sacks, which Peter imagined were filled with grain and other dry goods, and a flat stone the size and shape of a small, round tabletop. The space smelled of earth, livestock, and youth.

On his knees at the stone, the boy poured a pale-yellowish liquid from a rust-colored earthenware pot into two clay cups and a small bowl.

He served the men the cups, keeping the bowl for himself, and then piled a grain sack on top of another at the table and used it as a chair. "Drink, Pedro. It is rude for the host to go first."

It was thin-bodied and harshly sweet, but not bad. Peter nodded a thank you to the boy.

"Chicha is made of Indian corn. This has no alcohol. Some," Aldo said, grinning, "is strong, make you happy." He took a swallow. "Sumaq," he said as he raised his cup to the boy, who lifted his drink.

Aldo said, "Pi manta?"

The boy replied in a strong voice that rose and fell as he put emphasis on certain syllables.

"His mother made the chicha, and he asked that I tell her he is well when I see her at his village."

It dawned on Peter that the boy was similar in age to Devon. "How long does he stay out here by himself?"

"As long as it takes for the llamas to get their fill of the grass in the pasture … maybe two weeks. There is probably another pasture up near the village." Aldo took a sip of tea and wiped the corners of his mouth with his index finger. "The variety of different grasses is good for the llamas."

"Ask him his name, Aldo."

Aldo lifted his chin toward the boy. "Ima suti?"

The boy looked from Peter to Aldo and then back to Peter. "Tian."

Peter tapped his chest and said, "Pedro." He offered his hand toward his guide. "Aldo."

"Ah," the boy said.

While they were drinking chicha, the boy answered Aldo's inquiries in increments—a short sentence or two, a pause, and then another response. It seemed he was recollecting the route, seeing a turn, which he would indicate with the hand off to the left, right, or forward. He used his hands when needed in conversation, but there was nothing overly dramatic about this boy. He said what needed to be said, and if a hand was needed to explain, then by all means it would be used.

There was a singular understated confidence with this boy, alone, living on a hillside with a herd of llamas and goats. Some current of a different type of life ran through him as if he had tapped into an atavistic vitality from these mountains. That, Peter thought, was why he was drawn to this boy and these mountains. This was a world where he felt alive unto himself.

Could one live a lifetime alone in these mountains? It seemed Yachay was, but were these Tian's formative years before he settled down with a woman in Olaquecha? If he did, Peter thought, he would have regrets about the unavoidable compromises. In the silence of the mountain there is much you can learn.

CHAPTER 13

Peter woke before dawn. Tian's bedroll to his right was empty. Aldo, lying next to him, slept on his back, gentle snores wheezing through his lips. Peter peeked out the door as the mountains showed in black silhouette.

He dressed quietly and went outside, where he found Tian striking a spark with a blade of flint on a flat stone, holding it over dry grass and twigs. Within a few sparks a thin plume of smoke swirled upward like a vaporous specter. A flame emerged, and the boy sat back, bringing his knees up to his chest, his youthful face aglow in the firelight. There was a haunting quality about him, like an elusive phantom of the night who might fade away at the first hint of dawn, never to be seen again.

From the corner of his eye, Tian had seen Peter when he emerged, but he had made no acknowledgment. And Peter felt no slight; it was not necessary.

By sunrise breakfast had been eaten, and soon after, Peter and Aldo were packed and ready to depart.

Tian raised his hand for them to wait. He removed a hand-woven pouch on his hip and placed it on the table. "Kru puriy," he said.

"Coca leaves," Aldo said, "for our journey."

"Agradisikuyki," Peter said. He placed his hand on the boy's shoulder. Tian's eyes, wide set and alert, met Peter's gaze, and in it he felt as if he were looking into the soul of these mountains.

Peter thought of the old man in the little desolate village where they had bought gas. He seemed to live in limbo between two worlds—the mountains and civilization. Here, this boy had found his bliss. Yes, there were hardships with more in the future, but there was a confidence about this boy-man that he was in a good place.

* * *

Peter and Aldo wove their way through a narrow pass, then up one steep trail, and then another. The departure from Tian's place seemed long ago and the past two days like a long stretch with a variety of new experiences: awakening at dawn to the soft tremors of Yachay's flute, eating in the road, crossing the bridge of vines, meadow teeming with wildflowers, starkly beautiful lake with rock and more rock all around, meeting Tian and his llamas, and spending time with that intriguing boy. What more lay ahead? How much more could his body withstand?

"We must push hard while the weather is good," Aldo had told him more than once. But now the coca leaves had been spat long ago after Peter had drained their juices. Now he ached from the arduous trek.

They came to a patch of barren land littered with boulders, which looked out over a valley of scrub trees and rocks. The once-bright sun was now late in the western sky, the shiny day fading. Soon they would need to stop.

Peter straggled behind Aldo, who stopped and looked up the mountain like a dog finding a scent. "We must find better shelter for tonight. It will be cold. Can you walk more?"

Peter was so tired, so damn tired, he wanted to drop his backpack and sleep right there. His lungs were screaming for him to stop, and the fatigue was smothering his spirit that had gotten him to this point.

Again, Aldo looked up the trail and then back. "We must push, amigo, to make the most of the daylight."

Peter wanted to shout, Yes, you have told me that, but his mouth was too tired to speak. Then he felt pressure on the indentations, his mystery dimples as Deb called them, on his side and hip. It wasn't pain but as though a warm, gentle touch was encouraging him up the mountain.

"Pedro?"

Peter lifted his chin for Aldo to continue. On they walked.

Aldo had told Peter that an ancient ruin was not much farther. Damn, Peter wanted a coca leaf, but he would not ask.

At dusk, they came to the ruins of a village. Below them stone walls weaved around stone huts in no discernible pattern. A series of steps led into the village.

"You hungry, Pedro?"

"More tired."

"Bueno," Aldo said. "I find place for us to sleep. You wait here, uno momento."

Aldo investigated a couple of huts and then went up another set of steps to an arched opening into the side of the mountain. "Come, Pedro."

The sky was a gloamy purple, and some stars were visible, but Peter was too exhausted to admire them as he went to join his guide.

Their sleeping quarters were no more than ten by ten with stone walls and a stone floor.

"This is good," Aldo said in a weary voice. "We set up before darkness comes."

They ate cold potatoes and quinoa in silence. Peter had trouble chewing, his mouth seeming to fight every chomp and chew. The cumulative effect of three days' trekking uphill in high altitude, carrying a pack, had taken a toll on his body, and with it his spirit had flagged during the course of today's hike until he hadn't been sure if he could go on.

But sitting cross-legged in this small grotto, he had regained his metaphysical equilibrium. Earlier, when he thought he could go no farther, he had felt that sensation of warmth on the indents on his hip and thigh. At the time he was too tired to give it thought. But something unusual had occurred when his exhausted body had mustered an inner strength to go on. Where it came from, he did not know. The remainder of the uphill walk was a blur, but he had made it.

Peter packed away the uneaten food and took a sip from his canteen. Outside, night had fallen over the land and all he could see were the inexorable stone walls glowering in the shadows. The sight triggered a warning that he needed to keep his guard up, that he should not let his newfound self get carried away with the moment. In Tian's countenance, when they sat at the fire earlier this morning, there was a look of vigilance that said, I am where I belong, but it is a difficult life, and I must be on guard.

There was something old and wise about that shepherd boy as if he had lived many past lives and had learned many things. And from that boy, Peter ascertained that vigilance was a good skill to have while living in these mountains.

CHAPTER 14

Peter rubbed the heavy sleep from his eyes with the heel of his hand as the first glimmer of morning entered the stone grotto.

The events of the past few weeks ricocheted inside his head, from getting his death sentence from the doctors to the radio show on shamans, which he had heard only because a headache forced him to pull off the road. Then there were the meetings with Neil Judd, John Vander Bosch on the plane, and Aldo. Was he a pawn in the hands of fate, only to be laughed off the mountain and humbled back home to his death? Or was this some magical moment in the hands of destiny? He felt destiny at his side.

Before his illness, he would have sneered at these occurrences as mere chance. The pragmatic architect Peter Richards would have never believed such nonsense. He thought back to the meeting with the civic association about the construction of Ebert, Heiden & Richards's new office building and a point he had emphasized, "I for one do not believe in myth. I have the art and science of architecture on my side."

He had played that role perfectly, and at the time he believed what he said. He remembered the dissenting expression on the old hippie woman's face, a wise and kind face with a look that said there were still things for Peter to learn. How right she was.

The old Peter Richards would have gotten chemo and all the rest of it and died a horrible death. That man now seemed far away from this enigmatic, timeless land. And death didn't loom over him as something to fear but as something inevitable.

He sat up and saw Aldo's bedroll empty. He ran the tip of his tongue over his lips and noted them swollen and a bit sensitive. His cheeks felt flushed, and he rubbed his hand over his stubbly unshaven face. He imagined he looked rather weather-beaten from the wind and sun. But it was good to have reached this point, not only the outward journey but the one inside Peter as well. Each incremental challenge of the trek up the mountain that he had met had given him strength for what might lie ahead.

Peter walked down to the middle of the ruins and looked around. Pointy-topped rock formations rose up at the promontory's edge, beyond which sunlight peeked out between brown-green mountains, their peaks veiled by misty clouds. In some parts, the clouds parted, revealing the first hint of blue sky. At the other end of the ruins were the steps leading up to the trail. Filling in the rest was the ancient village of stone. The walls that he had thought meandering had an artistic, serpentine curvature that separated the huts into private enclaves.

He walked around the ramparts, one behind the other with a terrace of wild grass in between. The architect in him admired the quality of the tight seams between these massive stones. Was this another step to learn from these ancient structures? Another clue that would encompass more than a search for a cure?

"Pedrooo, are you up yet?"

Peter stepped back into the path at the sound of his guide's voice. He saw Aldo coming down the steps from the trail, empty-handed. "Good morning, Aldo."

"You sleep like niño, no?"

"Yes, I slept well. No wood?"

A thin smile creased Aldo's lips as he made his way toward a long rectangular stone. "Bring my pack over. We eat cold food once again." He stepped up onto the stone and spread his arms out. "But we eat under the watchful eye of el cielo azul."

Aldo raised his hand to the sky, now a striking azure as though a giant eraser had wiped it clean, and then he turned to Peter. "Backpack, pronto. We eat and take advantage of our good fortune." He raised his eyebrows in a shrewd, appreciative manner, his keen eyes smiling and appraising at the same time. "You have come far in our journey."

"Seems far," Peter said, "but there remains a ways to go yet."

CHAPTER 15

After a couple of uneventful hours on the trail, Peter and Aldo came upon two boys, around twelve years old, coaxing a herd of llamas down a path off the trail to a terraced corral of moss-green grass bordered by a stone wall. At the far end of the corral were three lean-to shelters equally spaced apart, thirty feet or more in length.

The llamas moved in an orderly fashion, turning off the trail onto the path. Some had coats not as thick as the others, and Aldo said they most likely had been sheared a month or two ago. Peter wondered if this herd alternated with Tian's. The boys, wearing knitted caps, tapped any lingerers along on the rear with walking sticks.

Aldo said the grass was called ychu grass and provided different nutrients than the long grass and wildflowers below.

"Those niños are about my age when I first visited my mother's village."

They stood a few yards from where the llamas turned off the trail.

Peter saw a glimmer of admiration in his guide's eyes. "Tell me about your mother's village, Aldo."

"Ah, Pedro," Aldo said with a particular tone of remembrance, "I will never forget the awe and inspiration that day when I discovered a missing part of myself meeting my mother's family—uncles, aunts, cousins, and my grandfather Quayo."

Aldo told Peter that he had heard from a fellow guide that his mother's village had erected a couple of shops that sold blankets and pottery and the like. "This village, Olaquecha, no doubt has remained true to its roots and history."

After the last of the llamas had moseyed onto the path, Aldo approached the boys and spoke to them in the Indian tongue. The boys kept looking at Peter, who smiled reassuringly at one and then the other. The taller of the two boys looked up the trail for a moment and then answered Aldo in a few words. He then asked the boys another question, and their inquisitive expression turned reserved as they nodded in unison. Aldo spoke again, and the boys exchanged a glance. Then both raised their shoulders—*we don't know.*

"What did they tell you, Aldo?"

"The village is not far, and the shaman is not there at the moment." Aldo raised his hand before Peter could interrupt. "That is all they could tell me."

Peter grasped the front straps of his backpack and raised it up his back. "Let us go," he said, "and wait for this great shaman."

"That is the spirit, amigo."

The trail wound around a bend, and shortly after, they came upon the village, situated on a jut of rock and hard earth. To their left, thatched-roofed adobe huts lined the perimeter in a half-moon arc. Aldo motioned Peter to follow him over to their right.

They looked over a wide and half-as-deep terraced hillside with a series of earth-and-timber steps descending to a patch of level ground before a sheer drop-off overlooking a valley.

A variety of crops, from leafy plants to root vegetables, grew in neatly spaced rows all the way down the hillside. Villagers were digging out of the ground, with wooden trowels, strangely shaped tubers colored red, yellow, purple, and even candy-striped. Some were as round and bright as billiard balls, others were long, and some were wrinkled. And placed at intervals along the rows were woven baskets to collect their yield.

Aldo looked toward the colorful vegetables being harvested. "Those are the lost crops of the Andes, Pedro, grown by the lost people, the Cloud People. And," he said with a trace of pride, "it seems they like it that way."

"Lost crops?"

Aldo said, "Uh-huh," as his mind seemed to drift back in time. "Yes, it is called oca or uqa in Quechua, and I haven't seen it since I was a boy." He grinned and made a gesture with his chin. "Look below—quinoa."

The last three rows on both sides of the steps were spiny plants with stems rising at the tips, standing anywhere from four to eight feet high.

"I read back home that it is similar to pigweed plants."

CHAPTER 16

Peter stayed back as Aldo approached an open-air thatched-roof structure supported by timber poles and a back wall made of straw and mud. In the middle was a high-legged table where two women were mashing grain with wooden rolling pins. Behind them was a cluster of earthenware pots, each strung from a wooden tripod over hot coals, and along the back wall sat bags of grain and wicker baskets brimming with potatoes and the colorful oca.

One of the women was heavyset and in her late thirties, the other slender and in her early twenties. Both had black hair in pigtails.

The older woman looked up, squinting as though looking for a lost article. Her intense gaze remained on Aldo as he greeted her. He spoke again, and she replied, "Qhari wawa, Tian?"

"Tian allin maqt'a." There was a harmonious singsongy tone in Aldo's voice like a mountain minstrel delivering good news. He then chatted amiably with the woman, no doubt telling of the time spent with Tian.

Peter approached, and both women looked at him as if witnessing something unexpected. He raised his hand in greeting and then said to Aldo, "Is she Tian's mother?"

"Yes, she is very happy to hear her son is well."

Both women appeared captivated by Peter's arrival, looking him over from head to toe.

"Tell her how much I like Tian."

The woman leaned her head forward with keen interest.

Peter grabbed Aldo's arm, his eyes on Tian's mother. "Tell her he is a special young man."

Aldo told the woman, who blushed with maternal pride.

"Agradisikuyki," the woman said.

112

After a momentary silence, Aldo cleared his throat and said, "May Shaman?"

"Oh," the older woman said, an expression passing over her brown face that was a mixture of reverence and strain.

She then replied to Aldo, who then asked a few more question before thanking her.

Aldo steered Peter a few steps away. "She says he will be back sometime today." Aldo glanced at Tian's mother with a spark of admiration. "This evening the shaman will lead the ceremony for a native holiday."

"Are we welcome?"

"It should be okay." Aldo folded his arms across his chest, his eyes busy in thought. "The shaman … his name is Pavor … when he returns, we will know then." Aldo's attention was diverted momentarily as Tian's mother stole a peek at him. "It appears the shaman is hombre grande in this village. What he says," Aldo said with an indifferent shrug, "is the law."

The younger woman came over and motioned for them to sit at a long rough-hewn table along the outer edge of the cooking hut.

Peter sat in a wood-framed chair with the seat and back made of tightly woven vines. It was sturdy, as was the table, which was assembled by all wood joints and wood fasteners, without a nail or screw—the same as his desk at work. He gripped the table edge. It appeared old but strong. The architect in him admired this way of construction, which allowed the wood to move with seasonal shrinkage and expansion, giving it a much longer life span. Nails and screws hold the wood too tight, eventually leading to cracks. This table could last as long as the wood held up, a thousand years or more, Peter thought, as the younger woman served him a bowl of an oatmeal-like substance.

She then handed each man a wooden spoon.

Aldo said to her, "Sulpáy."

"Imamanta," she replied.

"This is gruel," Aldo said before digging in with gusty slurps.

It was rather bland, but it felt good to Peter to get warm liquid down his throat. "Is this made of what I think it is?"

"Yes, more potato, Pedro." Aldo lifted an eyebrow toward the women and said in a raised voice. "Or as the people here say, ulluku."

The women looked up from their task of scraping coarse potato meal into a large bowl with wooden spatulas. The older one smiled toward Aldo before they both returned to their task.

Peter turned in the direction of the sudden bleating of an animal, but he saw nothing but a string of adobe huts, their faded ocher façades glistening in the sunlight. "Is that a goat I hear?"

Aldo looked up from his dish, his gaze on an animal hide hanging from a rope along the back wall. "Yes, they provide leather, milk, and meat. There is probably a goat pen behind the huts."

"These people … are they completely self-sufficient?"

Aldo scraped the last of his gruel onto his spoon. "It seems that way. They are far from civilization up here in this land among the clouds." He placed his spoon in his mouth and held it there for a moment, savoring his last bite. "And, my friend, they like it that way. They live much like their ancestors did." He folded his hands on the table and sighed. "And as mine did also." He then took his bowl over to the women. The younger woman kept a respectful distance while Aldo and Tian's mother exchanged playful banter.

As Peter finished up the last of his gruel, he thought of how timeless this rugged world was … the blue mountains rising into a cluster of billowy clouds, the thin but pure air he breathed, and the people tending their crops on the hillside. Peter noted the women as Aldo visited with them, their expressions placid, without a bit of stress or strain. He imagined them content in this difficult life. These people, these endurers, lived in their own time, speaking their own unique language, in a world unto themselves.

But he considered Aldo's words that the shaman was the big man here. And Peter had ascertained that Yachay was none too pleased with whatever rules these villagers lived under.

"Napaykullayki."

Peter wheeled around in response to the sharp voice to his rear, and to his surprise, no more than a foot from him stood a man in his fifties, dressed in a collarless brown shirt and sandals. Stealth-like, this short brown man with squinting eyes had come upon Peter undetected. His stooped shoulders and obsequious manner indicated this could not be the shaman.

The man stared up at Peter as if he was some rare species, and then his gaze turned querulous as he leaned his head forward, inspecting the red poncho as though looking for defects.

Aldo came over and greeted the man, who replied in a tone of one introducing himself and then relaying instructions from a superior. Aldo listened and nodded, occasionally asking a question. When he was finished, the man bowed his head to Aldo and then to Peter.

"What was that all about, Aldo?"

"It appears, amigo," Aldo said, "that Penne, here, says your arrival was expected."

"What do you mean, expected?" Peter said. "Who expected it?"

"The shaman."

CHAPTER 17

Penne said, "Hamuy." He then swung around and walked across the village square with Aldo and Peter in tow. He moved as though his feet barely touched the ground, like a predator stalking its prey.

At a hut across the square, Penne pushed open a door similar in design to the wide-plank tabletop where they ate, but with cross-braces running diagonally from the corners. He stood at the entrance as though not ready to allow access. Penne spoke to Aldo, putting special emphasis on the word *munay*, which he said twice. And each time he said the word, his eyes darted over toward the women in the cooking hut.

Aldo raised his hand in thanks. The man bowed his head to Aldo, and then to Peter, and left. "If we need anything, Penne says we are to ask the women at the cooking hut," Aldo said as he glanced around the village, "and if they can't help, they will find someone who can get us what we need."

"How about that," Peter said, "room service."

Aldo laughed a deep, hearty laugh and said, "Yes, amigo, room service and in the ático. What is the word," he said as he flicked his finger, "ah yes, the penthouse. We are living on the top floor."

One persistent question that floated in Peter's mind was, how could the shaman be expecting him?

Aldo seemed to read him. "Be patient, amigo," he said in a carefree tone. "The difficult part of the journey is over. Now we must wait patiently."

There were two windows in the front of their hut, with rawhide flaps rolled up and tied above, reed mats and blankets were on opposite sides of the space, and stationed above each mat was a torch in a dadoed slot in the wall. A table with two chairs was in a corner, and that was it. This was Peter and Aldo's sleeping quarters on orders from the shaman, Pavor.

"I could use a siesta," Aldo said as he dropped his pack on a mat.

"I think I am going to look around, if that's okay."

"Okay?" Aldo looked up from spreading his bedroll over the mat. "The big honcho has been expecting you, and now that you are here," he said through a soft chuckle, "I am sure that everyone in the village knows."

"Good enough, then." Peter raised his hand to Aldo, who was already under the covers.

Peter left his poncho hanging on a hook near the door. A nudging voice suggested leaving Havo's gift inside. There was something in the way Penne had eyed it that he couldn't explain but left him a tad uneasy about wearing it in the village.

On the hillside, villagers continued to tend to the oca, while a few others snipped leaves off the coca plants, storing them in woven bags. Peter noted that the quinoa was not tended.

The men and women went about their business as though they had been doing it all their lives ... and well they had, Peter thought. Conversation among these people was at a minimum, a word or two here and there. But mostly they seemed to communicate with nods and looks. There was a quietness about these people living in this remote village hidden high in sky.

He wondered what the shaman would look like. He would most certainly be an older man, at the very least fifty. Would the first sight of him instill confidence, or would he think him ordinary like Penne? He thought the former.

Peter looked off in the distance—the mountains crowded the sky; everywhere mountains in their silence of stone.

He wandered around the village checking out the construction of the adobe huts. The corners were reasonably straight, as were the mud-filled joints, but this workmanship's size and scope were nothing in comparison to those of the ruins.

The faint bleating of goats reminded Peter of Tian. He wished he had inquired when the boy would return to the village. A pang of guilt registered when he thought of his son and wondered how he was doing with his father far away in search of a miracle cure.

But he had a deep-seated sentiment that Devon had turned a corner and made friends in the astronomy club. Possibly they met each day during lunch in the cafeteria to chat about the stars and even other things, like girls. A faint thought whisked in his mind—how great it would be to stargaze in the backyard with Devon's astronomy club.

Debra would be pleased about that, Peter thought, as the image of her in the kitchen rose in his mind, her apron with the yellow-and-red flower pattern tied evenly in the back, looking out the window, fighting her worries about her husband thousands of miles away, out of touch—

The *bah, bah* bleat of a goat brought Peter back to this terra firma, which seemed to exist in another dimension, another universe, as if Portland were another lifetime. He was not who he used to be. He had begun this trek in search of a cure for brain cancer, and though it was always in the back of his mind, something else was taking up space. He was on an inner journey to discover a new Peter Richards. *Give it time,* he thought as an overwhelming weariness came over him.

Back at the hut Peter found Aldo sound asleep. He made a pillow out of the blanket provided and lay down on his mat.

* * *

Peter heard a faraway voice. "Pedro, come and see." He felt a hand on his shoulder. "Wake up."

He sat up in his bedroll, heeling his hand against his eyes. "Boy, I was out."

"Come and see."

Aldo extended his hand, which Peter clasped, and he stood. "What is it?"

Aldo went to the door and waved him to follow.

An old man wearing a gray poncho was coming into the village leading a llama loaded with a bundle covered by a blanket. The man's gait was steady and strong, belying his age.

A boy ran up and took the reins. The man glanced at the strangers, his face as creviced as the Andes, revealing nothing. He walked to the cooking hut, where the younger woman had returned. She placed a bowl of gruel and a plate of cheese on the eating table, her eyes following him until he sat. He tilted his head toward her as if to say, that is all. He took a spoonful of the gruel and then paused before taking another, looking straight ahead, a mountain monarch alone with his thoughts.

This man had gravitas. This man seemed capable. "That's him, right?" Peter said. "The shaman, Pavor?"

"I am sure it is. We will wait."

After finishing the food, the old man raised an eye to the young women, who removed the bowl. He put both hands on the table and stood; then he turned and approached the strangers.

"Come, Pedro, let us meet him."

As the man neared, Peter thought of Geronimo. There was a wild fierceness glistening in his wide, deep-set eyes that seemed to belong to another century.

The old man looked at Peter, his eyes bold and unblinking. He then spoke to Aldo in a low, rumbly voice. It was a voice of authority, of one in control. When he finished, he looked at Peter and then turned and walked away.

He crossed the village square like a land baron inspecting his property, a look here, a look there, the sharp eyes missing nothing.

When he reached a hut across the square, he looked back at the visitors. Even from a distance of fifty yards, an aura of power and confidence resonated from him.

"He says we are to join the ceremony tonight."

Peter looked at Aldo. "And ... ?"

Aldo lifted an eyebrow and gave a look that Peter had come to know.

"I know, be patient," Peter said. "Be patient."

"Yes, Pedro," Aldo said as he scanned the village with a look of someone finding something unexpected, something that had been missing.

* * *

By dusk, a group of men in red-and-blue checkered tunics formed a circle in the middle of the village square. They extended their arms so that their fingers touched. Pavor emerged from his hut, and Penne handed him a wooden pole with a carved head on the top, which he carried in front of himself. He approached the circle of men, looking straight ahead, his blank expression revealing nothing, but the watchful look of respect on the faces of the men left little doubt as to who was in charge.

The remainder of the villagers circled the men and the shaman.

The shaman said in a deep guttural voice, "Padura kutiy, Padura kutiy, Padura kutiy …

"What's he saying?" Peter asked Aldo.

Aldo remained silent.

"Hampiy Padura, Hampiy Padura, Hampiy Padura …"

"Aldo, what does Padura mean?"

"In due time, amigo."

Pavor raised the pole overhead, looking up at the night sky.

"The shaman is paying his respects to the Granary. The siete hermanas. The pole is a go-between to the spirit world."

"The Seven Sister, Pleiades?"

"Sí. Each man in the circle asks a sister for a good sign."

Peter counted the men. Seven.

Aldo raised his hand to the sky. "The brighter they are, the better the rain. Not bright, dry."

Pavor handed the pole to a woman attendant and then raised his hands high to the heavens.

"Maia Mea, Maia Mea …" The shaman kept his head up toward the sky, his voice gaining power. He repeated the chant three times and then lowered his head. The silence of the shaman seemed to emanate from him through the villagers and then into the night air.

From a small leather pouch on his hip, the shaman sprinkled a white powdery substance on his palm, which he raised to the sky.

Pavor lowered his palm and blew the powder into the air. He chanted again, reversing the words, "Mea Maia, Mea Maia, Mea Maia." The shaman raised his hands overhead, palms upward. "Padura, kutiy."

The villagers hummed, "Ohm." Pavor raised his hands out to his sides, palms remaining upward. "Padura," he said with emphasis, *Pa Dur Rah.* Then, the villagers trilled in singsongy unison, "Yah, Yah, Yah …" Three men began banging with hand-carved sticks on cylindrical drums, made of wood slats and animal hide, in a repeated rhythm, *"Bom, Bom, Bom … Bom, Bom, Bom …* The people swayed their shoulders back and forth.

Aldo whispered to Peter, "This is their annual ceremony of thanking the gods for their crops."

Peter scanned the southern sky, locating the Pleiades. But they were upside down from what he was used to seeing in the Northern Hemisphere.

"Aldo, since I was ten years old I have been fascinated by that cluster of stars." He raised his arm overhead, pointing to the Seven Sisters, twinkling like royal jewels. "And now I am here seeing them inverted in the Southern Hemisphere."

The banging of the drums continued their rhythmic beat, which seemed perfect for observing the stars. Why that was Peter did not know. He leaned over to Aldo and said, "As a boy I used to dream about the Pleiades being positioned upside down." He realized that what he was about to say could no longer be denied. "It's as though the Pleiades and my destiny are intertwined."

The drums stopped. Nobody moved as the shaman raised his head back and then clasped his hands together over his head.

"Yes," Aldo whispered as he watched the villagers stand very still around Pavor. "The Granary holds many secrets about one's destino."

"Do you know I haven't felt ill since we began this journey?"

"There is magic in these mountains."

"It is very strange."

"Do not rush these things, amigo. Let it come."

Pavor clapped his hands like a headmaster dismissing class, and the villagers began dispersing.

Peter turned from a tap on his shoulder to find the stealthy Penne. He bowed his head to Peter and then Aldo, to whom he spoke.

"Pavor asks that we join him in his hut," Aldo told Peter.

"Let's go."

They found Pavor's hut empty. It was similar in size to the other huts in the village. There was a straw bed on one side and a table and chair at the other end. It measured no more than two hundred square feet but, much like his hut, the circular sparseness made it appear larger.

Pavor entered followed by four elders, including Penne. At the center of the space, the shaman leaned down on one knee and then the other. One of the men tried to help, but he waved him off as he leaned back and crossed his legs, hands on knees. The elders sat facing Pavor in a semicircle. Torches on the adobe walls cast an exaggerated confluence of shadows and light on the faces, adding an aura of mystery to the scene.

Pavor swept his hands out for Peter and Aldo to sit with the others. They sat to the shaman's left, Peter on the end.

A short-stemmed wooden pipe was lit and handed to Pavor. The shaman looked at Peter and then at Aldo. "Nahuatl pastu?"

Aldo leaned toward Peter and said, "Pastu is a mix of dried secret herbs. He wants to know if we will join them."

Peter nodded. "Allin."

Pavor took a strong pull and then passed the pipe to his right. It had a wide face with steep cheeks and an aquiline nose carved on the bowl colored with red-and-brown earth tones. It appeared to be very old.

Peter inhaled deeply as the others had. He coughed and coughed again. Whoa, this stuff was powerful. The pipe made three trips around.

The pastu put Peter in an altered state but different from the marijuana of his college days. The effect was more powerful and mind-altering. He felt extreme peace coupled with awareness of everything around him.

Pavor folded his arms across his chest and spoke to the group in a measured voice but with power and conviction. The elders listened intently. He was telling a story not just with words but also with his gaze, which bespoke of an innate intelligence passed down through generations.

When Pavor finished, Aldo leaned over to Peter and said, "He says your arrival is good sign for his people."

"What else did he say?"

"He says there is more for you to learn."

Pavor spoke to Aldo in a short burst.

"He asks that you remove your pants, Pedro."

"What?"

Aldo motioned for Peter to stand.

Peter took off his boots, stood, and removed his pants.

"Yanapay," Pavor said in a commanding voice. One of the men helped the shaman up to his feet. He lowered the elastic band on Peter's briefs and tapped the indentation on his hip with his fingertip. "Yah." He looked at the elders, his eyes saying, it is so. He raised Peter's shirt and touched the other indentation below his rib cage. "Padura, Padura," Pavor said in a husky voice. The elders chanted, "Padura, Padura."

Peter looked at Aldo and said, "What or who is Padura?"

"In time, amigo," Aldo said, raising a hand for patience. "We must not rush these things."

The shaman motioned for Peter to sit, and then returned to his sitting position, again waving off assistance. He tipped his head to the elders on one side and then the other and said, "Ripuy." The elders departed the hut single file, each bowing his head *good evening* to Peter. In their gaze there was a look he had not seen before, a look of respect. Pavor extended his hand toward Peter for him to wait. The shaman then lifted his chin toward Aldo and leaned his head in the direction of the door.

"Pedro, you stay." Aldo departed without looking back.

There they sat facing each other: the shaman and the stranger.

Pavor closed his eyes and tilted his head back slightly. He sat very still, hands resting on thighs, like someone in deep mediation.

Peter closed his eyes, still feeling the powerfully calming effects of the pastu. He drifted into a gentle form of half-awake consciousness.

They remained in this position for a good ten minutes before Pavor said, "Maki." Peter opened his eyes and saw Pavor with his hands turned palm up. Peter did likewise. The shaman leaned forward, taking Peter's hand in his. His touch was sandpaper rough. He traced Peter's lifeline with his fingertip and nodded in confirmation. "Allin."

Pavor folded his arms across his chest, his ancient eyes on Peter. Those deep, dark eyes—what secrets did they hold? "Allin tuta, Padura."

Peter took it to mean he was saying good night but was calling him, Peter Richards, Padura. Again, who or what in the world was Padura?

Back in their hut, Peter found Aldo already asleep, stretched out on his back under a blanket.

Peter got into his bedroll. The effect of the pastu was wearing off, and with it came an edge of uncertainty. It had been a long day, from finishing the trek up the mountain, meeting Pavor, the ceremony to the gods of the Earth, and the pastu powwow. Sleep would not come right away. There were things to consider, such as the word *Padura* that he had heard during the ceremony and when Pavor had inspected his indentations on his body. "Padura, Padura," the old man had said. Was Pavor saying that he was somehow connected to someone named Padura? And how did Pavor know to pull up his briefs to reveal his indentations?

And seeing the stars inverted at the ceremony just as he had dreamed as a child … had this other world, Padura's world, attempted to reach him in his upside-down childhood dreams of the Pleiades? How real those dreams had seemed, but once he was awake they would quickly fade from his conscious mind.

And what was he to make of the fact that ever since he had started the journey up the mountain, he had not had one headache or even given his cancer much thought? What was going on there?

And why was it he had thought little about Devon and Debra? He felt a quiver of guilt before his practical side realized that without embarking and concentrating his efforts on this transformational journey it would all be moot, for he would soon be dead. And he realized he still might die. But there was something in these mountains that gave him hope—not just the shaman but something mystical.

Finally, he grew sleepy. Yes, it was time to surrender for now, for it had been a long day, a long and intriguing day. As Aldo would say, do not rush these things, for in the silence of the mountain there is much you can learn.

CHAPTER 18

In the morning, Peter found Aldo at the cooking hut, and he took a seat across from him. "Mariaqua," Tian's mother said to Peter, tapping herself. A smile spread across her broad face, revealing a hint of the beautiful girl she once was.

"Good morning, Pedro," Aldo said pleasantly. "Join me ... goat cheese and bread." He lifted his chin toward a clay platter with a stack of flatbread and a log of chalky-colored cheese.

Mariaqua placed a hand on Aldo's shoulder, leaned over the table, and put a plate in front of Peter. He broke off a piece of cheese and placed it on the bread, doubling it over. The sweet chewy flatbread complemented the strong, tangy cheese. "I know I am supposed to be patient, but what is going to happen today, Aldo?"

Aldo took a nibble on his cheese and wiped the corner of his mouth with his thumb. "Pavor will tell us more when he is ready."

"Come on, Aldo, you know more. I saw it in your eyes last night at the powwow."

Mariaqua came to the table. "Aswan, Padura?" She stood at Aldo's side, hip brushing his arm.

Aldo said, "Anything else, Pedro?"

Peter offered a little shake of the head to Mariaqua. He said to Aldo. "Well?"

"All right. Pavor dreamed the other night that the reincarnation of a great man of these mountains from long ago would arrive in need of his help—"

"Wait. Are you telling me he thinks I am—"

"Padura," Aldo interjected. "He is saying you are the living spirit of a heroic leader from many centuries ago." Aldo raised his hand. "That is all I know except that Pavor is waiting for another dream with further instructions."

Peter glanced at Mariaqua, her eyes gleaming respectful admiration upon him, her hand once again on Aldo's shoulder. "I have come far on this journey," he said as he put his hand on his chest, "but that is a lot to comprehend."

Aldo nibbled on a torn piece of bread. "You need time." He raised his hand with a flourishing sweep and brought it to rest atop Mariaqua's. "Walk around the village," he said, "the hillside, and off on your own." There was a sparkle in his eyes of one anticipating a big event about to occur.

"All right, then."

"Allin, Padura," Mariaqua said as if she understood the gist of the conversation.

* * *

Peter stood at the top of the steps overlooking the terraced hillside. Below him, three pairs of men and women were at work, each pair in a separate row. The men were digging into the soil with tall, thick sticks attached by rawhide straps to a sharp stone plate. Above the plate was a piece of wood that was used as a foothold.

As the men dug, the women sifted through the upturned earth to reveal a plethora of potatoes, which they loaded into wicker baskets. The teams worked in rhythm: dig, load the basket, and step to fresh soil. The women, in colorful skirts and sweaters, were barefoot, and the men, in knee-length trousers and ponchos, wore sandals. In one pair was the young woman from the cooking hut yesterday. He figured the man with her was her husband. Though they didn't look at him directly, Peter felt the charge of their awareness of his presence, which they didn't acknowledge as though giving him space.

There was a dignified serenity about these quiet people. Peter felt not a stranger who had intervened into their world, but one who was welcomed.

Did they also think he was the reincarnation of this great man, Padura? And how was he great? *Slow down,* he told himself.

As Peter made his way down the hillside steps, cutting through rows upon rows of crops, their watchful eyes followed him.

At the bottom, below the quinoa bushes, was the level area that had a breathtaking view of a green valley, endless sky, and deep gorges between mountains ... always the mountains.

Off to his right was a wide cantilevered cliff that banked around a bend backed by a sheer of rock. He stepped toward it and stopped. He looked up at the pickers, who had all eyes on Peter. In their watchfulness there was respect and even concern. Peter raised his hand to them. "Allin." *I am good.* One of the men returned the gesture, and then they returned to their chore.

Sitting cross-legged on the cliff, his back against the rock wall, Peter realized how far he had come. A year ago he had been an organized, detail-oriented architect with a full and happy family life. Then earlier this year he had become moody and sullen. Now he was transforming into someone different, in a remote mountain far from home in search of a miracle.

A key to this miracle led to Padura. Could he have possibly been him? He told himself to remain patient, wait, and listen. Also, to stay vigilant.

A dark spot disappearing behind the tail of a long silver cloud caught Peter's eye. Another eagle? The spot emerged from the cloud heading toward him. He made out a black, broad-winged bird with a white-ringed neck. As it neared, the size of it became clear.

It was huge, twice the size of the eagle he had seen with Aldo and Yachay. The bird soared, circling a swath of air, rising and falling with the currents. It was a condor, passing so close that Peter made out a purplish waddle of skin in folds under its neck and a brownish-red eye. It flapped it massive wings once, whooshing like a bellow from a blacksmith's forge.

It continued its arc away from Peter until it disappeared from sight. He started to analyze the significance of this event but stopped.

Let it come, he told himself. His breathing slowed as he entered an inner state of acuity. He must remain patient, not fight his impulses ... just let it come.

His mind drifted away from its present view into a state that Peter could only describe as nothingness. It seemed a place where time did not exist, a place unencumbered by the physical world, a place so vague yet so clear ...

When he came out of it, he was once again aware of his surroundings. Beyond the mountains, the sun arced toward the center of the sky, right about eleven thirty, the same hour he would observe from his office window the old gentleman meandering his way—one step forward, lead with cane, bad leg out to side—to his park bench.

How different this world was from the old man's. He wondered if he wouldn't have enjoyed gazing out from this ledge at the vastness with book in hand ... looking up every so often and appreciating the solitude and beauty. High up in the land of the sky, whatever demons Peter had imagined the old gent had suffered might have been allayed to some degree. What did he think about when he smoked that one cigarette each day after finishing his sandwich? Was he thinking, what if, and blaming himself for some series of events in which he was a helpless pawn?

How fortunate he had thought of the old man for at least having lived an entire life, and how he, Peter Richards, was getting shortchanged. Now he realized the falsehood of his thinking. He was the fortunate one to have lived a rich and prosperous life, with a good woman and blessed by a son. *It will be grand to see them again,* Peter thought, *but first things first.*

He creaked his way to a standing position. His muscles were sore. But he felt healthy, not like someone who had been diagnosed with a terminal illness.

Peter came upon the young woman from the cooking hut with her man, sitting at the bottom riser of the long steps sharing a steaming bowl of what Peter surmised was boiled quinoa.

"Tiyay," the woman said to Peter. She spread her hands in front of herself for Peter to sit.

He sat on the ground facing them. They were a fine-looking pair, both dark-haired with high cheekbones like the shepherd boy, Tian. But they were missing the untamed quality that radiated from every part of Tian's being. These people seemed accustomed to living in the village under the shaman's command, while Tian gave off a vibe of independence, that of a person in search of something more.

"Napa ..." Peter tried to remember the word for hello.

The girl laughed. "Napaykullayki." She offered her hand for Peter to share their food with them.

Peter did remember his vocabulary lesson from Aldo when he wanted to thank Yachay. "Agradisikuyki."

An appreciative smile flickered on the young man's face. "Quinoa." He lifted the bowl toward Peter.

Peter reached in with one hand and pulled out a handful. With the other, he spooned some in his mouth. "Allin," he said between chews. It was soft and smooth on the palate and left a pleasant aftertaste.

After eating, Peter thanked them and started for the steps but stopped to inspect a quinoa bush. Silvery flower clusters were sprouting at the base of some of its leaves, which were turning a violet red. He stepped into the row for a closer look.

"Quinoa mana kamarisqa."

Peter turned to the sound of the young man's voice.

The man touched a leaf and then made a falling motion with his fingers. He raised his finger to indicate there was more. "Wayta," he said as he repeated the falling motion. His eyes said, Are you with me?

Peter nodded hesitantly as the man ran an open fist down the side of the flower with the open palm of the other hand at the bottom as if to catch what fell. "Ahhh," Peter said. He got it. The leaves fell first, then the flowers, and then the quinoa seeds remained to harvest. He rubbed his stomach and said, "Quinoa allin."

A wide smile split the boyish face. "Quinoa allin," he said, pantomiming Peter's rubbing of the stomach as if he had just discovered a new trick.

After leaving the crops, Peter wandered about the village, stopping to watch two barefoot girls standing on a large flat stone stomping a large pile of potatoes, which considering how easily they were mashed had most likely been boiled.

They were talking and laughing quietly until Peter neared. He raised his hand in greeting. "Napa kull ..." He couldn't get the hang of that word.

"Napaykullayki," one of the girls said in a shy voice.

Peter smiled a thank-you and then motioned for them to continue. They exchanged glances for a moment and then stomped with the heels of their feet as moisture squirted out of the small round potatoes. Aware of Peter, they worked silently. When they finished, they squatted down, each with a thin piece of wood shaped like a ruler, scraping the chunky mash into a pile in the stone's center. Then they grabbed each other's hand and stomped over the remains. Little giggles emerged from their lips as the joy of this task seemed to override the presence of a visitor.

As Peter turned from them, a few steps away the giggling grew louder and then there was a burst of girlish laughter.

Outside the village perimeter, the only sound Peter heard during his walk was an occasional riff of wind. He discovered the goat pen down a short trail at the rear of the village. The pen was barricaded by a stone wall a tad lower than Tian's llama corral. He counted twenty-three goats of various coloring from white to splotched brown and gray.

At the far side of the goat pen, he found a narrow rocky path. After zigzagging for a couple of hundred yards, he came out at the far end of the llama corral he had first seen on their arrival. It was empty, and Peter wondered if they had been taken down to the pasture where Tian was. Or could there be other pastures nearby? There was a simple efficiency to this village called Olaquecha. But interspersed with this life was the shadowy aura of Pavor, which seemed to shroud every aspect of this mountain hideaway.

He headed around the corral toward the main trail, which he and Aldo had arrived on. Halfway there, he discovered yet another trail or, more accurately, a swath Mother Nature had cut between two hillsides. The path led to where the two hills converged in a *U*-shaped rise that met the horizon. It was more of a challenge than Peter felt like taking on, and also the sun was arcing down the western sky, casting shadows over the hills. It was time to head back to the village.

At the cooking hut, a woman was shucking corn while another was skinning a goat carcass hanging by its back legs. Nearby, a large pot of water sat on stacked logs awaiting ignition. Two other women pounded water-soaked long grass with rounded wooden clubs. One of them then mashed it into a pulp while the other took it into long strands between her dexterous fingers. No movement was wasted.

When they had arrived in the village, the sight of a boy doing this chore had captivated Aldo. But that was not the only thing that seemed to have drawn his guide's attention. He wondered what was going on between Aldo and Mariaqua: the hand on the shoulder, hip brushing his side, and the exchange of flirtatious glances. But didn't she have a husband? She didn't act like it. Maybe he was dead, or who knew, Peter thought as he watched a circle of boys, in the middle of the village, playing a game with a ball of twine, kicking it back and forth, trying to get it out of the circle.

When Peter neared them, the boys' laughter fell silent. As with the girls on the stone it was as though their parents had told them to be respectful of the stranger.

"Pedrooo." Aldo was standing outside their hut with shoulders square and hand over head like a tourist on his first day at a resort.

"How did your day go?" Aldo said to the approaching Peter.

"Quiet, very quiet."

"Ah, you are learning." Aldo looked off for a moment and said, "Did you see or feel any inspiration?"

"Well, I did a form of mediation on a cliff below the crops."

Aldo said, "Bueno. Anything else?"

"Walked around the village, and … oh yeah," Peter said, wagging his finger. "I saw the biggest bird, a condor, soaring out of the clouds when I was sitting on the cliff."

Aldo's lips crimped in a quizzical twist. "What was its color?"

"Black, except for a white band on its neck."

Aldo exhaled a slow stream of air like someone hearing big news. He looked at the sky where Peter had seen the bird. "In the southern sky, you saw the black bird?"

"Yes, does it signify anything?"

Aldo's gaze remained steady on the sky. "It is a good sign, a very good sign, when one sees an eagle in the north sky, as you did with Yachay and me, and in the southern, El Condor." Aldo looked back at Peter. "As I told you, there is magic in these mountains."

"When the condor flew near me, it flapped its wings, just once, and the sound, so very distinct, was like a *whoosh*." Peter glanced in the direction of the hillside. "And after the condor disappeared from sight, I fell into a very relaxed state where it seemed hardly any time had passed."

Peter stared at the ground and said, "And when I came out of it, much time had passed."

"That is because you are letting go, Pedro." Aldo clasped his hands together and said, "And becoming one with all around you."

CHAPTER 19

Peter and Aldo stood outside their hut, each in deep contemplation. The late afternoon sun cast long shadows across the village square.

Aldo broke the silence. "Tonight, the village feast."

"Is it for what I think it is?"

Aldo said, "Yes, for the return of Padura."

Everything about this journey Peter could accept and even welcome, except the unfathomable idea that he was the incarnation of some past ancestor.

"Also, Pavor left early this morning to consider."

Peter stared at Aldo. "Consider?"

"His dream."

"Aldo, tell me what you know."

A matter-of-fact smile skipped across the guide's face. "He will tell us tonight after the feast." Aldo looked over toward the cooking shack and caught Mariaqua's eye. He raised his hand to her and received a warm smile in return. "So get some rest, amigo," Aldo said as he started for the cooking shack, "and the evening will arrive soon enough."

* * *

Peter stirred from a restless nap at a bonging sound. He got up and put on a knitted sweater shirt and went to the door. In the shadowy fading light, the adobe huts glowed from torches stationed around the perimeter, bringing to mind a village in a globe, its own private world.

In the village square, a group of men, seven Peter counted, were banging on the cylindrical drums in a constant *bong, bong, bong.* Again, seven men were playing an important role in a village ceremony ... possibly a connection to the seven stars in the Pleiades?

As dusk settled over the village, a long splash of purple streaked the horizon. In front of the cooking shack, women were placing bowls, one after another, on a row of tables. On the tables were a huge bowl of some sort of stew—Peter figured it was from the skinned goat—steaming quinoa, stacks of tortillas, and bowls of a variety of mashes. No doubt one was from the girls stomping on stone.

Villagers were coming out of their huts over to the drummers bong-bonging away. The women were dressed in bright skirts, mostly red with zigzag patterns above the hemline. Some carried toddlers on their backs wrapped in large rectangular cloths worn over the back and knotted in front, and all wore large bowl-shaped hats with a zigzag design on top. The men were dressed in ponchos over collarless shirts, with dark shin-length trousers.

Aldo approached Peter and they exchanged glances. There was a look of ancestral pride in the guide's eyes. "Here he comes, Pedro."

Pavor was heading over to the drums, wearing a woolen cap with a high stack and floppy rim, but what caught Peter's eye was the red poncho Pavor wore, similar in every way to his own, with the same bright-red color and rolled collar. There was not another poncho close to this style.

The shaman's gait was steady and sure as he cast an authoritative look of satisfaction upon the villagers like a monarch overseeing his realm. He came to a halt in front of the drums, projecting confidence that Peter was receiving loud and clear.

The villagers formed a ring around the shaman and the drummers. Pavor raised his hands. The drums stopped. "Qilqa Viracocha, Qilqa Viracocha," Pavor said.

Aldo leaned over and whispered to Peter, "He has received a message from Viracocha, the Creator."

Pavor clasped his hands together in front of his face. There was silence for three beats, and then the shaman commanded, "Hamuy, Padura."

Aldo said, "Go to the shaman."

Peter went into the circle and faced Pavor.

One drum beat *Bom ... Bom ... Bom ...*

A cup filled with a chalky-colored liquid was handed to the shaman. "Upyay." Pavor handed the cup to Peter. He took a sip and grimaced. It had a strong, bitter taste. "Upyay llapa," Pavor commanded. Peter took a gulp, swallowed, and then another, finishing the drink.

Pavor put his hand on Peter's forehead, rubbing it in a circular motion. The hand grew very warm, and the warmth filled his chest and extremities. Peter felt light-headed, as if he had entered a state of extreme inner peace, drifting away from his conscious mind and the physical world. Time seemed to stop, or better yet, he felt as though he were in a place where time did not exist: a place of solitude, a place of grace ...

Peter felt Pavor push against his forehead with the heel of his hand, bringing him back to the here and now. Pavor stepped back from Peter, who felt a burning sensation flash inside his skull like kinetic fireworks followed by a warm glow flushing his face.

The drum stopped beating, and the villagers surrounded Pavor and Peter, and in unison they hummed, "Ohmmmm ..." Once again, Peter grew light-headed, his body ethereal. He couldn't explain it, but he felt cleansed on the inside as though Pavor's touch had triggered—dare he think it—his healing.

Pavor began a rhythmic, garbled chant. The only words Peter understood were *Padura* and *Viracocha*, which the shaman emphasized. When he finished, Pavor swept his hand out to his side, indicating for Peter to rejoin Aldo. He spoke to the villagers for a minute, and then his lips parted in a half smile of composed satisfaction. "Qallarly raymi."

A cheer came from the villagers, reminding Peter of fans at a sporting event when the home team won in the last seconds.

"He says the festival has begun," Aldo told Peter.

"Am I healed?"

"In a while we are to meet with the shaman in his hut."

"One more thing," Peter said. "How long did the ceremony take?" Peter turned to Aldo.

Aldo smiled, his expression that of reverence, of someone who had witnessed something rare. "Ah, maybe an hour."

"Wow," Peter said. "Wow."

Again, Peter fought the urge to question Aldo any further, as his inner voice requested patience.

The festival was a joyous occasion with the men drinking a stronger, alcoholic version of chicha. Peter took one sip that reminded him of a very potent grain alcohol. The food was tasty, especially the goat stew, which Peter had a second helping of.

At first, the people kept a respectful distance from Peter. But as the night wore on, the men drinking chicha—and it seemed they all were— approached Peter with celebratory expressions and slurred words.

"Padura, imamanta." *Welcome, Padura.* Some even embraced Peter, and many more patted him on the back, as if he were a returning relative after a long time away.

With the festival still going strong, Pavor summoned for Aldo and Peter to join him in his hut. Under the haunting, flickering torchlight, they sat cross-legged in a circle. Pavor spoke in short guttural bursts with Aldo translating.

"Viracocha came to me in my sleep before your arrival. He is everywhere in these mountains." Pavor lifted a hand over his head. "You have seen the eagle and El Condor." Pavor looked at Aldo and grunted as if to say, You have told me this is so. *"When El Condor of the south flies with the Eagle of the north, it is good sign for Quechua people."*

Pavor reached over and put his hand on Peter's knee. "The moment you set foot on the mountain, Viracocha was watching over you. He kept your illness at bay while providing good weather for your journey."

The shaman leaned forward, his eyes on Peter as Aldo translated.

"I removed your illness this evening." Pavor rubbed his forehead with his palm. "You, Padura, are healed."

A sense of utter relief washed over Peter. But also remaining was the question if there was more to this than his healing. And finally, the old Peter's voice echoed in his mind: *Am I really cured?*

"Agradisikuyki, Pavor." Peter bowed his head in thanks to the shaman.

Pavor looked at Aldo like a boss man prepared to give orders. Then a word was said and left to hang, "kutiy," and then another, "musqhuy ..." A total of ten words. The shaman made a walking motion with his fingers to Peter.

"He said tonight there are some words I need to teach you. For tomorrow he will guide you up the mountain to a special location."

Back in their hut, Aldo wrote on a notepad the ten words and their meanings. "You study these." He then smiled a carefree smile as he turned to a rumble of laughter coming from the village square. "Do not wait up for me tonight, my friend." He kicked back his chair and stood. "I am going to drink some chicha and spend time with the lovely Mariaqua."

* * *

A tapping sound woke Peter from a deep sleep. He sat up in the darkness and heard another *tap, tap*. He got up and went to the door. There stood Penne in the dawn light.

"Pavor puriy." Penne drew the words out in a heightened tone of importance.

From Aldo's notes Peter knew *puriy* meant hike.

Penne tapped his chest. "Suyay," he said as he bowed his head. He was going to wait, no doubt on orders from Pavor.

"Okay," Peter said as he noticed Penne looking out of the corner of his eye at his red poncho hanging on the hook. He turned to Aldo's bedroll and found it empty. "Son of a gun," he said under his breath as he reached for his boots.

CHAPTER 20

Pavor led Peter around the llama corral to the path between the two hillsides. The shaman walked with purpose in his step, shoulders straight, elbows at the sides, arms churning him forward. Less than a quarter of the way to the *U*-shaped rise, Peter took note of two stone façades, with heavy planked doors built into the hillside. "Pavor," he said, making a walking motion with his fingers toward the doors.

The shaman squinted at the doors and then up the trail, his expression revealing nothing. "Yah," he said as he stepped off the trail.

The first door they entered opened to a room a good twenty yards into the hill and half as wide. Workbenches ran along both sides. It seemed as though they had stepped into an ancient assembly-line factory. One side had baskets filled with llama wool followed by ceramic bowls containing colored dyes, behind which wooden combs and brushes hung on the wall. Another section had spiraled wooden pins, and last was an array of sewing pins and hand looms constructed of a series of sticks and thread.

On the other side were stacks of the finished products with skirts, ponchos, shirts, and trousers all stacked in piles. Peter went down one side and then up the other, stopping to admire the craftsmanship while Pavor waited at the door.

The other space, not far from the first, was a similar setup but used for woodworking. An impressive display of stone and wood tools—awls, knives, hammers, axes, and other tools—hung on the walls.

Back outside, Pavor brought his hands out in a sweeping motion onto his chest. "Sapallan." He leaned forward toward Peter. "Huh?" He raised an index finger and clutched it in his fist. "Sapallan," he repeated as he brought his still-gripped finger to his chest.

"Yah," Peter said, nodding. "Uh-huh." He understood it to mean that they were self-sufficient, one for all. But, Peter thought, this self-sufficient world was ruled by one ruler, Pavor the shaman.

Past the *U*-shaped rise, they made their way up rocky terrain that Pavor managed like a spry mountain goat. They were now on the opposite side of the mountain that Peter and Aldo had trekked up. As they continued upward, the valley below grew smaller, the clouds seemingly within reach. Peter couldn't fathom what the old shaman had in mind, taking him up here. What could this have to do with Padura and the past lives? He smiled to himself. It wasn't any use asking due to the language barrier, and even if they could communicate, Peter knew Pavor well enough to know he would not reveal anything prematurely.

Everything about Pavor had a deliberate air that said, Do not hurry. Take your time to understand the situation and take the appropriate steps to reach your goal. And what was this wily old man's goal? He stated he had cured Peter, the reincarnation of Padura. Okay, fine. What more did he want from Peter?

At their first meeting, Pavor had brought to mind a man overlooking his personal estate—a man who got his way and one who wasn't likely to take no for an answer. Peter had a gut feeling that he would soon be saying no to this shaman.

For a couple of hours, they walked in silence, Pavor leading the way over trails similar to the ones Peter had encountered on the journey to Olaquecha. It was a bright sunny day, the air brisk, but hardly a breeze stirred—perfect conditions.

Pavor came to a halt when the trail ended at a rocky plateau overlooking a wide valley with swatches of grassland running through craggy mountains. The shaman stood still, hands at his sides, looking below on the valley. Ahead and to their right were sheer drop-offs, and on their left was a rocky incline.

The shaman turned to his left and said, "Kutichiy ta tapuna, Padura."

Peter understood from Aldo's vocabulary lesson, *Here is your answer, Padura.*

Where? The incline was at a forty-five-degree angle and appeared insurmountable.

At the base of the incline, a pair of boulders met in a lazy *X*, so that only their middles touched, leaving a small opening at the bottom.

Pavor got down on his knees and reached into the gap, stretching his arm out until his shoulder could go no farther. Out of the dark space emerged a wound braided rope. He knotted a loop, looped the open end through it, and made a lariat. He uncoiled the rope in his left hand and took a position directly underneath a ledge twenty feet up. Below the ledge, a pointed-tipped spur of rock jutted out of the hillside, projecting toward the sky. Pavor allowed the rope to slip and the noose to grow larger, as he swung it over his head three times before taking a step forward and casting the noose toward the rock—bull's-eye. He tightened it around the base of the rock and pulled himself up.

The old shaman scaled the incline like a veteran mountain climber. Who was this man? And where was he going?

When Pavor reached below the spur, he stepped up onto a shelf of rock to his immediate left and dropped the rope. Standing waist-high to the ledge, he then shimmied himself up.

Peter tugged the rope to test its strength. There was no give in it. He was surprised by how easy it was to reach forward, pull, step forward, and climb. At the top, he did as Pavor had done and got himself onto the ledge, which varied from three to four feet in width.

Pavor gestured for Peter to follow him toward the valley side. He did not want to end up with only the valley below. Walking on a narrow ledge with a fifteen-foot drop was one thing; doing it with a two-mile drop was another.

They came to where the ledge wound around the mountain to the valley side. Pavor stopped and looked over his shoulder. "Ama karu," he said.

Not far? Peter raised his hand; he needed a minute.

"Padura," Pavor said in an avuncular tone. Everything about him radiated kindness, from the wide-eyed look of anticipation to the easy shrug of the shoulders, his aura of power replaced by that of benevolence. It seemed this old shaman could wear many masks.

What the heck? He had made it this far. "Allin," Peter said with all the gusto he could muster.

Hugging the mountainside, Peter focused his eyes straight ahead on Pavor's back, not daring to look down. One careful step and then another. After a couple of minutes, Pavor came to a halt.

When Peter caught up, Pavor was standing before a large opening into the mountain, a cave. He brought his finger to his lips—don't tell. Peter crossed his hands over his chest.

Inside the cave, the shaman removed a torch from a hole in the wall near the entrance. He handed it to Peter and then took out a rawhide pouch from an interior pocket in his poncho. He pulled out a piece of flint and a striking rod. From another pocket, he removed a pouch containing what looked like lard. Pavor smeared the substance, which had a pungent odor, over the bark wick and then sparked the rod and flint on the wick. On first strike, a flame emerged. It seemed that the lard controlled the flame. Pavor took the torch from Peter and entered into the darkness.

Farther in, the light flickered eerily off stalactites dangling from the jagged walls and ceiling, creating an aura of shadowy otherworldliness. Peter didn't see any beams or braces; this was a natural cavity in the mountain. They entered a half-moon opening into a chamber. Along a back wall was a crude etching of a stick figure of a man standing atop a circle.

Pavor ran his finger around the circumference of the circle. "Kay Pacha," he said. *Earth.*

The figure held a wand directed toward a cluster of specks over his head. The specks—seven in all—were positioned like the Seven Sisters of the Pleiades in the Southern Hemisphere. Below the Pleiades was a smaller stick figure tethered to a line down to Earth. Pavor put his finger on the figure standing on Earth. "Viracocha," he said. Then he raised his torch up to the other figure. "Padura."

Was Pavor telling Peter that he was the incarnation of a starman, Padura, from the Pleiades and that long ago Viracocha had summoned him to Earth? Even for the stripped-down version of Peter Richards, this was a lot to believe.

Pavor tapped Peter's sternum. "Kunan p'unchay sapa maskhay." *Today you search inside yourself.* He put his hand over Peter's heart. "Padura kutiy." *Padura has returned.* Then he put his hand on Peter's temple. "Ch'isiman, Padura." *Tonight, Padura.* He raised his index finger and looked at Peter with a stern yet paternal look that said, Be patient, for there is more for you to learn. "Intindiy?"

"Intindiy." Yes, he understood. And he would be patient for whatever the night would bring.

The walk back was uneventful other than their seeing Penne and some other men entering the woodworking hut along the trail. Peter wondered if Penne didn't have two jobs, Pavor's gofer and woodworking.

After walking Pavor back to his hut, Peter passed some village men sitting at a table in front of a hut drinking chicha. They were having a grand time in their reserved way, talking in muffled tones that occasionally erupted into low laughter, faces animated with joy ... still celebrating the return of Padura, no doubt.

Aldo and Mariaqua were at the cooking shack sitting at the long table, holding hands. He was whispering sweet nothings in her ear, while she acted like a young girl on her first date. It struck Peter how much that fine man had sacrificed for him, scaling this mountain and staying at his side every step of the way. *Enjoy, Aldo,* Peter thought. He would follow Pavor's instructions and spend time alone with his thoughts.

On a high point near the empty llama pasture, Peter took a seat on a rock to reflect on his journey: Havo at the mountain base, his trek with Aldo, meeting Yachay and Tian along the way, the healing ceremony, the Pleiades, and the cave with the drawings. It seemed as though each segment was a stepping-stone toward enlightenment that he *was* the reincarnation of this starman Padura.

Peter thought of what his doctor, Bob Goodman, had told him right before he left. "I have feeling, Peter, a sense, that you may be a stranger in your own world who must go out into it and find your true self." Had Peter discovered his true self? He sat crossed-legged facing the distant mountains. He let his mind drift past the here and now.

He snapped out of his reverie at a loud *cluck, cluck* and then a shrill hum. What an unusual confluence of sounds. Up the trail, Tian was bringing his llamas into the pasture. Peter stood on the rock and hollered, "Imamanta, Tian."

The boy looked up, a glimmer of recognition in his eyes, as he raised his hand to Peter. "Napaykullayki," the boy said before turning back to his flock. He gripped a long stick that he used to tap the buttocks and flanks to keep the llamas in single file as they clomped and snorted their way into the pasture.

The sight of Tian sent a rush through Peter, not only at seeing him again but about his own son, Devon. An undeniable urge ran through him to be in the backyard with Devon stargazing, Peter telling him about the sky in the Southern Hemisphere. And Debra must be a nervous wreck, not having heard a word, probably wondering if he were still alive.

Peter sat back down on the rock, realizing his mission was not complete yet, and that his yearning for his family and to visit with Tian were human frailty. He must see this thing through.

The landscape below was a hardscrabble mixture of rock and earth, the view more desolate than from the terraced hillside of the green valley. He looked out to the mountains in the distance, brown and vague, and lost himself in a semiconscious state, drifting once again into a harmonious mind-set of nothingness, an otherworldly place where the senses were useless.

At dusk, Peter came out of it. He felt a subdued energy of prescient awareness that told him he was cured. Simply cured.

* * *

The village was quiet and still, save a couple of shadowy figures over at the cooking shack. "Padura," said a female voice from the shadows. Peter found Mariaqua and Tian sitting at the table eating quietly. A smile spread across her broad face; her boy was home.

Tian looked up from eating. "Quinoa." He offered his hand to a chair across from him. Peter sat, and Mariaqua quickly set up a plate of food. They ate in silence, but it felt good to be in the presence of this independent man-child. Might this boy roam, never calling anything home but these mountains? There was a discrepancy in his mother's glowing face—in her eyes a shadow of concern for her boy as if she realized his fate.

Peter ate his food and left. He found his hut empty and wondered if Aldo was waiting at Mariaqua's hut, giving her time alone with her son and also Peter, per Pavor's instructions.

On his bedroll was a pipe packed with pastu and a pack of matches. Peter struck a match and drew deeply.

CHAPTER 21

Dreamworld

In a time long ago, through the eyes of the great eagle soaring over an Andean valley, a green land with tiers of stone structures separated by walls comes into view. Weaving through this village are thoughtfully placed paths and steps, also of stone. A terraced hillside emerges from the mist, brimming with rows of green leafy plants. A man, Padura, leads a woman and a boy to a hut.

As Kamachiq, leader of the village, Padura should feel confident, for the Pleiades have shined brightly during the short winter days to signify mild weather and plentiful rain. But there is a faint stirring in the air suggesting that change lies ahead.

The woman, who has black hair and chiseled beauty, is Paca. The boy, Pacura, has his father's noble features, with an aquiline nose, cleft chin, and hair like dark grain in a gentle breeze.

From an early age, Padura was told he was different from the others. His father, whom he had never met, made him so.

His young, growing mind sought knowledge about the stars, especially the Pleiades and their influence on his people. He learned the craft of cutting stone and erecting structures that endure the shaking of the earth when Viracocha is displeased, and building tables and chairs that last for a thousand years by using only the materials that the trees offer, and the secrets of the knotted strings, Khipu.

The elders took him from his mother as soon as he could walk to begin his education. By the time he had grown tall and strong, he was noticeably larger than the other boys and even the men. Padura was on his way to becoming Kamachiq.

But before that could occur he must solve the mystery of his father's identity. His birth was unusual—mystical, he was told. One day his mother, a virgin girl, woke up with a swollen stomach, and soon after Padura was born on that eventful night.

Padura pondered this conundrum. For three days and nights, he slept little trying to understand how he came to be. He considered the seven days prior to his birth when the Seven Maidens of the sky disappeared behind the moon, only to appear again after he was born.

Finally, he concentrated on the Pleiades and Viracocha, the Creator, who arose from the stone mountain during the time of darkness and brought light.

Viracocha first created brainless giants that he destroyed with a flood. He made smarter, smaller ones—Padura's people.

Finally, in a dream the answer came that Viracocha had gone to the Pleiades to get a distant perspective of his new creation. Yes, they were better than the mindless giants, but to be safe he needed to have his own progeny among them. Viracocha picked out a young virgin girl and one night went to her room as mist. He entered through her nostril and stayed the night.

Padura went to the elders and told them that Viracocha was his father. "And how did you know this?" Padura was asked.

"That is for you to determine."

The elders looked down on their young prodigy. "You have come far, Padura. It is your time."

Since that time, prosperity and good health stayed with Padura's people. Their crops were plentiful, and each year Padura led a ceremony to thank the Seven Maidens for their good fortune.

But for some time his stars had disappeared from the night sky. A knot tightened in his stomach, like wet Khipu being stretched. Padura sent maskhays out to search for any signs of activity in the valley below.

The maskhays met tall men of bronze skin who had journeyed across vast waters and walked long distances. Their language was in a strange tongue, so they communicated with the maskhays with their hands. They were brought to the village, stayed seven days, and enjoyed the effects of the coca leaf.

During their visit, the bronze men taught Padura how to store events of the sky with braided ropes, which were like the Khipu but thicker and stronger, and their system for counting that used ch'usaq and huq—zero and one. This was the first knowledge Padura had ever received beyond the teaching of the elders and the gifted working of his own mind.

Viracocha came to Padura in a dream and warned of consequences of allowing outsiders to live among his people and sleep with the women.

When the first of the illness struck, over half the villagers found their skin erupted in boils filled with yellowy-white pus, bringing complaints of weakness and sore muscles. Some had spots on their tongues and fell terribly ill.

In the end, all of the elders and old people died, and over half of the remaining villagers. Those who lived had scarred bodies and faces. Pacura died, and Paca was no longer beautiful. Padura had only two signs of the illness, a scar on his hip and another on his side. He felt ashamed that his people had suffered so and that he had been spared.

Heartbroken from the loss of Pacura and many of his people, Padura decided that never again would his people be touched by the disease of the mana riqsisqa—strangers.

He went with his maskhays on a trek high up the mountain. After much searching, he found a secluded land that would be a difficult journey for any mana riqsisqa.

By the first snow, Padura had worked tirelessly leading the clan to erect earth huts and till the newfound land. But an early blizzard stopped all activity, and there was little food for winter. By the first thaw, many had died, including Paca, who had never recovered from their son's death.

For the remainder of his life, Padura devoted himself to his people. Over many years, his people's numbers grew. During that time no strangers had discovered them, nor had any illness struck his people.

Padura left this world just as he had entered. On the night of his death, the Seven Maidens hid behind the moon and did not appear again for seven nights. It was said that Viracocha forbade them from showing themselves until he had finished mourning. Thus the legend of Padura was passed on for many generations that someday his spirit would return and never leave the mountain again.

* * *

"Padura, Padura. I am Padura," Peter said as he struggled to wake. It was as if the dream didn't want him to leave its world. Through blurry vision, he made out a figure sitting crossed-legged on the floor.

"Padura," the voice said in a gentle, fatherly voice—the shaman's voice.

The old man spoke to Peter, making circular gestures with his hands.

The only word Peter understood was *Viracocha*. An image of Paca and Pacura in an Indian hut rose in his mind. They looked sad and disoriented. Standing atop a mountain, the giant of stone, Viracocha, raised his staff, and pale-blue light descended over the hut. "Live on the mountain, and in your dreams we will join you," Pacura and Paca said in unison. "You will never be lonely."

Peter ached to go back to sleep and once again be Padura and with his family. Yes, he would lie back down and never wake and live for eternity with his first family.

A familiar voice shattered Peter awake. "Pedro, do you now understand?"

Aldo was sitting next to Pavor.

The pastu from last night had had a powerful influence on Peter, as if he were under a spell. He raised his hand to give himself a minute.

Clearheaded at last, he was flooded with a longing for Devon and Debra. He wanted desperately to get back to his family. He sat up, and in the shaman's gaze, he saw expectation. "I understand that Padura lived a difficult, honorable life. He was a great leader," Peter said.

Pavor's eyes narrowed as though he knew what was coming. He leaned his head toward Aldo, but his gaze remained on Peter as he spoke.

Aldo said, "He says that you will be an honored member of village."

The room fell silent, and the silence lingered in the air like an invisible entity.

Pavor spoke in a commanding voice.

Aldo said to Peter, "Viracocha came to Pavor in a dream. He will grant me safe passage to leave the village."

"And if I go?" Peter made a walking motion with his fingers to the shaman and said, "Puriy."

Pavor's wrinkled brow furrowed in an emphatic *no*. He lashed a finger at the guide, his words those of a parent scolding a disobedient child.

Aldo said to Peter, "Our good fortune on our journey was Viracocha looking after us."

Pavor sat cross-legged with his arms folded across his chest, his posture that of one demanding a satisfactory answer. He looked at Aldo and then at Peter. *"Huh?"* he grunted.

"No," Peter said.

The shaman extended his arms toward Peter, palms down, and crisscrossed his hands to indicate he was done with him. He offered his arm to Aldo, who assisted him in standing.

Pavor made the walking movement with his fingers. Keeping his eyes on Peter, he made a chopping motion on the fingers with his hand. "Wanuy pi urqu," the old man said before departing the hut.

"Just so I am clear, Aldo," Peter said, "if I leave with you, there will be bad things for us on our journey out."

"Sí, muy malo. Very bad."

"Aldo, you leave tomorrow, and I will depart three days after."

"Pedro, we need to talk."

CHAPTER 22

Peter and Aldo sat at the top of the steps of the terraced hillside, overlooking some village men scattered among the rows of crops. The men worked with meticulous care, bending and stooping, light on their feet as they hoed and weeded with hand trowels made of stone with wood handles, their nimble hands never stopping from the task at hand. They were subdued, shy, knowing they were being watched. Faces that had been alive with innocent happiness during the festival now had a look of uncertainty. These simple, decent people seemed to have an innate intelligence in deciphering a situation through an extra sense that alerted them to change in the air.

A swirling, cool breeze swept across the hillside, bringing a chill to Peter.

Aldo took a long, deep breath and sighed. "I have come to a decision that I would like to discuss with you."

The expression on Aldo's face was tight-lipped, the likes of which Peter had never seen from his guide. "Yes, Aldo."

"I want to live with Mariaqua." Aldo raised his chin in the direction of the plot of coca leaves. "She is what I need at this time."

Peter had missed her before, but there was Mariaqua, by herself, trimming off sections of coca branches and placing them in a basket. She peeked out of the corner of her eye at the two men at the top of the hill. It was a pensive look, a look with many layers.

"She is one of the few allowed to harvest the coca plants," Aldo said. "Pavor only wants those who know when to cut and where to cut."

Peter asked, "Are you taking her back with you to Lima?"

"No, I desire to live here."

"Here?" Peter said. "Do you think you can live as these people do?" He brought his palms up in front of himself and lifted his shoulders. "Under Pavor and his ways?"

"When I first came here," Aldo said, looking over his shoulder at the half-moon string of adobe huts, "it brought back memories of my mother's village." There was a gritty tone of certainty in his voice as if there was no turning back. "I want to return to my roots. Maybe someday, if she will allow," he said, offering a hand in Mariaqua's direction, "I will take her to the city and let her see." Aldo leaned forward, forearms resting on his thighs, and said, "I understand Pavor and his ways. He will allow me some leeway—Mariaqua told me so. But first," Aldo said in a changed tone, "I must get you down this mountain safely."

"Does she have a husband, Tian's father?"

Aldo straightened up and said, "Yachay, the wanderer, is Tian's father."

Peter felt his jaw drop. "Of course, we should have seen that."

Aldo proceeded to fill Peter in on more tidbits. Yachay had once come to the village years ago and met Mariaqua. He was a roamer, not a full-time wanderer at that time, coming and going as he pleased. But Pavor did not approve. When Tian was born, the shaman insisted Yachay live in the village and become a member or leave. A smirk formed in the corner of Aldo's lips. "I do not have to tell you what Yachay decided." Aldo looked toward the mountains in the distance, which were shrouded by a blanket of clouds. "There is more." He told Peter that when they met Yachay on the trail, he had just come from Tian's hut. "Do you know where he was going, Pedro?"

Peter brought a hand under his chin and rested the elbow on his forearm across his torso. "We have met three people on our journey who are different."

A knowing smile creased in the corner of Aldo's mouth. "Yes, amigo, he was going to see Havo." He raised a finger, leaned toward Peter, and whispered, "There is more, much more."

"More?"

"Yes, my friend." Aldo told Peter that Havo was Yachay's father and thus Tian's grandfather.

Their attention was diverted back to the coca plants, as they saw Mariaqua talking with Tian: the taut, lean body, the black thicket of hair, and the proud countenance.

Aldo tilted his head toward Peter and said, "He told his mother that when he turns sixteen he will leave the village for good. His mother is sad, but she understands." Aldo lifted his shoulders in a conciliatory manner. "He promises to sneak back to visit her."

"I see where Yachay and Tian get their independent streak," Peter said. He observed the villagers in the garden. He wondered how much they already knew, and what they were ascertaining by those indiscernible currents of life that ran through them.

"So, there are three independent, strong-minded men of this mountain who are related."

"No, there are four," Aldo said as he stretched his legs out. "Havo is Pavor's brother."

"It's all making sense now," Peter said.

"Many years ago, Havo was el jefe of this village, and Pavor studied under the resident shaman." Aldo brought his stretched legs up and tapped Peter on his thigh. "They are separate things, chief and shaman."

Aldo went on to tell of a power struggle between the brothers when the old shaman died and Pavor stepped into the position. Aldo flicked his finger at the villagers in the garden and said in a soft voice, "They are like children and were frightened of his magic." He fell silent for a moment before continuing, "After each healing, Pavor became more difficult for Havo to control, until the shaman told the people he would leave if Havo did not."

The intensity of their conversation seemed to vibrate down the hillside, where each individual tuned in like a human antenna. "So they ran Havo out of his own village?"

Aldo made a short cutoff motion with his hand. "No. Not like that," he said. "They asked him to work things out with Pavor."

Peter said, "Let me guess. Havo decided he had had enough and left of his own accord."

Aldo nodded to indicate that, yes, you are right, and that that was all there was to tell. "So, my friend, I suggest we depart early mañana." Aldo stared into his hands and said, "If all goes well, we will make it back to

Lima, you go home, and I settle my affairs." He looked out from the corner of his eye toward Mariaqua and said, "Then I return here to her and a life like that in my mother's village."

Peter placed his hand on his guide and friend's shoulder. "It seems we have both taken a journey of the spirit."

CHAPTER 23

The Silence of the Mountain

In the muted light from a torch on the wall, Peter lay in his bedroll. His sleep had been sporadic as he reflected on not just his time on this mountain but his life since he had been diagnosed with cancer ... on who he had been before his illness, during it, and was now here in an adobe hut high in the Andes.

He believed fate had played a hand in his getting this far, from Bob Goodman encouraging him to embark on this journey, to Neal Judd, John Vander Bosch on the flight over here, Aldo, Havo, Yachay, Tian, and Pavor. Yes, even the old shaman for giving him a deeper understanding of himself through a past life as Padura, even if Peter was now persona non grata. The man had saved his life. He felt to the core of his being that he was cured, making him all the more determined to get home and share his miracle.

He thought back to the scene in the family room when he told his son of his cancer and the heartache he felt—that they all felt. How he wanted to hold his family in his arms and tell them how damn much he loved them.

But there was a stirring in his gut about the challenges that lay ahead on the journey back. But what choice did he have? To live out his life here? He had to get home.

He had learned many things about himself during his stay, but the time had come to depart. While trekking up the mountain, he had suppressed thoughts of his family, almost as if he were in some altered state of consciousness from the mountain spell cast on him. But now he ached to be with them, to hear the sounds of their voices, to be in their presence, to be a family again—his own family in this life. To hold hands with Debra, to feel her touch. And to spend time with Devon stargazing. It seemed liked a year since he had seen them.

Peter turned on his side and cocked his elbow on the ground with his chin in his palm. Aldo rolled over in his sleep onto his back. Gentle snores blew out of his lips. Where would Peter be without that good and faithful man—a man who had difficulties in his life with a son he never saw and the son's mother, who didn't love him. And now he was going to try once again to find love here in this other world.

There was a sense of fait accompli about Aldo, a glimmer in his eyes that said, I am a pawn in the hands of fate. *Maybe,* Peter thought, *we all are.*

He sat up and stretched. There was a chill in the air, but intermingled with it, the faint scent of smoke.

He peeked out the door, and in the middle of the village was a smoldering, flameless fire that sent choking puffs of white smoke into the black sky. It brought to mind smoke signals, and Peter had a strong feeling in whose direction they were aimed.

He slipped into his pants and shirt, laced up his boots, and looked to the hook on the wall where he had hung his poncho.

"My God," he said as he neared the fire, "he is ruthless." The remains of Peter's poncho were draped over a disintegrating wood cross. The once-proud red poncho had turned black-gray with faded red splotches. Peter kicked the bottom of the cross with the toe of his boot, bringing the poncho down in a smoky *whoosh.*

He felt a presence, a set of eyes watching. Peter scanned the village and focused on the far end. In the shadows was a figure. The figure lowered his head like a bowing servant, stooping the shoulders—it seemed almost apologetically—and then the shadow was gone, swallowed by the darkness.

Of course, the stealthy Penne, Peter thought as he turned to the patter of footsteps.

"It appears the shaman was busy tonight." Aldo came up to Peter and the dying fire. He offered a hand in the direction of Pavor's hut. "One last detail Mariaqua told me about the shaman, Pavor."

Aldo told Peter that when Mariaqua's great-grandmother was a girl, a special red poncho of the finest llama wool was made by the best seamstress to be worn by the village chief for special ceremonies. It was to last for many generations and bring good health to the chief.

All the chiefs since had lived long and healthy lives. When Havo left the village, he took it with him. Pavor, not to be outdone, had an exact replica made that he wore for big occasions such as when he healed Peter.

Aldo looked up at the first sign of dawn breaking along the shadowy skyline. "Let us pack and get down this mountain."

At first light, they walked away from the village. There wasn't a soul around to say good-bye. Aldo told Peter that Pavor had probably told the villagers not to go near those who walk away. "And will you be welcomed back?" Peter asked.

Aldo shrugged. "First let us get down this mountain. Then I will concern myself with Pavor."

At the head of the trail, they came upon Tian on his way to the llama pasture. "Allin samiyuq kay." He wished them good luck on their journey. He told Aldo that they were welcome to stay at his hut down the mountain.

"Kuka chuspa," Tian said. He removed a small cloth pouch from his hip and handed it to Peter. In it were coca leaves and slivers of lime. The boy raised his hand farewell and held it for a moment—*I am with you.* He then made his way on to the path to his llamas.

Past the llama pasture, the trail wound around a series of boulders, which reminded Peter of sentries guarding the secrets of the village of Olaquecha. The morning air was foggy and brisk with a feel of moisture to it. Peter had yet to see any snow other than a smattering on the sides of the trail, and this was very rare according to Aldo.

An hour into the downward trek, the mist and fog had dissipated and bits of sunlight peeked in and out from the cover of a tumble of massive clouds. *So far, so good,* Peter thought, but still he had a gnawing feeling in his gut that challenges lay ahead. What they were, he did not know and wasn't about to discuss. *Keep following Aldo,* he told himself, *and stay alert.*

By midmorning, snow began falling from an unpredictable sky now a dull gray. Aldo came to a halt and looked over his shoulder at Peter. There was a hard edge in his gaze. "We come to the ruins soon. We eat and then go on."

From the trail, the ruins looked different under a layer of powdery white, the intricate workmanship of the walls and structures hidden, as were the steps that they carefully descended. The pointy-topped rock formations at the edge of the promontory were now an opaque blur of bumps.

They ate quinoa and flatbread in the opening in the side of the mountain where they had slept. Peter remembered how tired he had been the last time they were here, but also how confident that providence was at his side. Now he didn't know what lay ahead. He wished he could dismiss Pavor's warning, but the old shaman of this mountain had powers outside the scope of the normal laws of modern science. That much he was sure of. He would not rest easy until they were in Aldo's car and driving away.

"We must get to Tian's hut before dark, amigo." Aldo stood at the opening chewing on a piece of bread, while outside the snow continued to fall.

Peter considered suggesting they wait out the snow in the cave, but he wanted to be off this mountain. And, it seemed, so did Aldo.

They came to the stretch of barren land that looked out over the rocky valley of scrub trees now buried under a misty blanket of white. Their visibility of the immediate area was manageable, but the mountains in the distance had faded behind the gray sky, which seemed to be closing in, ready to swallow everything.

The descent was less strenuous than the way up the mountain; Peter's only discomfort was in his knees, and it was tolerable. He could use a chew of coca leaf, but they had a limited amount.

One foot after another, they continued down the mountain. It all seemed so different from the climb up. The land and its secrets lay hidden under the snow that fell from the insistent sky. Were they working in unison, the land and the sky? Conspiring to prevent Peter from escaping, to make him turn back up the mountain and back to his ancient people?

On and on they trekked down the mountain, stopping only twice for water breaks. As the last of daylight was fading from the gloaming sky, they came to the rise overlooking a snow-covered clearing, the llama corral. "Ah, bueno," Aldo said. "We live to fight another day, amigo."

Tian's hut offered immediate warmth from the biting cold. Peter and Aldo got out of their wet clothes and changed.

"Quinoa and flatbread, Pedro, is our meal once again." Aldo put his backpack on the table and removed tin plates and the food. His demeanor, though still confident, had additional gravitas.

They ate their second meal of the day in silence. Peter recalled his dream after Padura let the strangers into the village and pestilence struck his people. A growing tightness in his stomach sent a shiver through him. It was exactly like what Padura had felt when the Pleiades had disappeared from the sky—an ominous sense that hard times lay ahead.

* * *

The creak of the door opening woke Peter. He sat up in his bedroll and saw Aldo closing the door.

"We have good news and bad news, Pedro."

Peter sat up and said, "Good news first."

"The snow has stopped."

"Okay."

"But it is cold and windy."

Peter went to the door and peeked out. A cold stiff breeze whistled across the land like a siren. But a red-streaked horizon was visible. It appeared the storm had passed.

They ate quickly and headed out. Past the llama corral, they swished through the long meadow of grass, now blanketed in white.

The snow was light and not much of an impediment on level ground. Past the rocky-walled opening, they came to the lake. The water, which had been a stunning azure blue, was like a blue-black midnight sky. It seemed that every increment of the way down, the mountain appeared different from before—not just the snow cover, but also his awe at the breadth and beauty that had been replaced by something intimidating.

Farther on, they came to the first of the switchback trails, where the snow wasn't as deep as at the higher altitude.

The sky had turned dark blue, and off in the distance they saw the inexorable mountains.

"We must be careful on these narrow trails." Aldo checked his watch and tapped it. "Aah," he said, shaking his head, "it is not working." He looked at Peter.

Peter looked up, located the sun, and was about to turn toward the north when he realized he wasn't sure which way that was. He tried to ascertain north. "I am a bit disoriented, Aldo." Peter turned to his guide and said, "Which way is north?"

Aldo looked at Peter and tilted his head to the right. "Here," he said in a flat voice.

"Oh, of course." Peter faced north. The sun was approximately halfway between sunrise and high noon. He raised his hand toward the center of the sky. The instant calculation of factoring latitude with the sun's position wasn't there. He divided the sky into segments with his hand. It seemed there was a blockage in his brain that prevented processing the figures for a precise answer. "I'd say it's about quarter of ten."

Aldo looked at the sun disappearing behind the tail of a long gray cloud. He remained silent, his gaze on the sky, revealing so little that it revealed much. Finally, he said, "Let us share Tian's gift."

After packing their cheeks with scraps of lime and coca, they set off on the first of the switchbacks. Peter stayed behind Aldo as they zigzagged their way down the mountainside. The coca leaves alleviated Peter's soreness in his knees but not his shock at his inability to calculate the time. And the marvelous sense of well-being the coca had provided on the journey up was not there. Much like the villagers of Olaquecha with their human antennae, Peter was receiving a vague pulse-like sensation from the land he walked on and the surrounding mountains, a feeling of gloom like that experienced by a soldier on patrol in enemy territory.

They took their time zigzagging their way down, swishing along much like cross-country skiers—one foot forward, slide-step the rear, one forward, then the next—hugging the mountain, away from the edge. Here, Peter told himself, he knew the dangers, to stay away from the edge and don't rush. Here, he was on high alert. Once through the switchbacks, he must remain vigilant.

At the end of the switchbacks they came to a level area. Below were the brown valley floor and the silver stream that ran near Havo's hut. It seemed so close yet so far, another world from the one he stood in. He thought how the eagle or condor could soar down and be there in a matter of minutes.

By the time they arrived at the swinging bridge, the temperature had risen and the snow was melting. But the floor of the bridge and the vine-latticed handrail appeared to have been chiseled from ice. Peter snuck a peek below. The walls of the V-shaped gorge were covered in icicles. The growling roar of the stream, the water cascading off the canyon walls, sent a bone-hollow chill through Peter.

Aldo removed his wet gloves. "I cross, and then you follow." He placed his hands on the rail and slid forward on the ice-covered bridge, one step and then another, hands remaining on the railing as he proceeded forward.

Peter watched intently as his guide carefully, so very carefully, made his way. He would be glad when they were both on the other side, slapping backs, laughing as they walked away from the bridge, packing celebratory coca leaves in their cheeks.

Aldo kept working his way ... three-quarters across, then another step and then another. He was almost there. Peter felt as if he were walking every step. He imagined Aldo on the other side, facing Peter and encouraging him along. *Come on, Aldo,* Peter said to himself, *get over there and guide me home.*

When Aldo was just a few steps away from the other side, a sharp gust, seemingly out of nowhere, rocked the swaying bridge. Aldo fell onto his backside. Then a ghostly, hollow roar of wind echoed off the canyon walls. The bridge swayed wildly, shedding icicles and creaking like a coffin door closing.

Aldo tried to get up to a sitting position, but the bridge was rocking violently as the wind picked up steam.

Peter heard a crack like a rifle shot, and then on the far end a timber truss began to lose its hold of the mountainside. Aldo fought his way to his knees and reached for the railing. He struggled to a standing position, only steps from safety, when there was another cracking sound, this time with a horrifying finality to it.

As Aldo steadied himself, the trusses broke away, and with that the bridge swung out like a trapeze. He appeared to stand there in midair for an instant, his back to Peter, before he fell.

In that instant, Peter felt he was in a surreal dream. *How could this happen? Aldo cannot die. Something will save him.* But nothing did. The fall was a good three hundred feet, and when he thudded face-first onto a large rock, Peter knew he was dead.

It hit him that Aldo hadn't screamed or said a word as he fell—in the silence of the mountain there is much you can learn. He had accepted his fate to die in the land of his ancestors.

Peter stood on the cliff edge, stunned and trembling. The wind disappeared as quickly as it had arrived. He looked up at the sky, now a haunting light blue, and screamed, "You bastard! You bastard. You bas—" Peter stepped back from the edge of the cliff.

He removed his backpack and took a seat on it. He had to keep telling himself he wasn't dreaming—that it was true. Aldo was dead. Yes, Aldo was dead. He brought a shaking hand to his lips and ran it across his dry mouth. He took a drink of water from his canteen. His entire body was shaking. He had to calm himself and think rationally. He considered working his way down to the bottom of the gorge, not only to pay last respects to Aldo but also to recover the supplies from his backpack. Aldo had carried all the food; the only things Peter had were coca leaves and lime. And if he did somehow get down there, could he get out?

The safer plan was to return to Tian's, where there were supplies. From there he would figure out the long way down the mountain or wait for the boy or Yachay. He was not, under any circumstances, returning to the village of Olaquecha.

He decided to rest for a bit and pay his respects to that good hombre Aldo Coreas. Peter removed a sliver of lime from the woven pouch and placed it in his cheek. He then followed it with a bit of coca. He sucked slowly and thought back to when he first entered Aldo's office in search of a guide, the incredulous look when Peter told of his illness and the journey he had in mind. But then Aldo's expression had changed as his eyes met Peter's, and to his surprise he considered him simpático. Aldo had said to Peter, "Do you believe in destino?"

How his spirit rose when he had replied, "I do now. I have to."

That was the first moment he felt destiny on his side. That first day, Aldo had the look of a businessman, maybe even a shrewd one. But when he got to the mountains, he took on the appearance of a man in his true element. *If he had to die now,* Peter thought, *Aldo would prefer his mountains.*

At the edge of the cliff, he peered down at Aldo's body, which looked like a rag-doll figure he had seen in one of the shops in Lima. "Adios, amigo." A shudder ran through him; he was on his own. *Stay calm,* he told himself as he tried to fight the jangled uneasiness that stirred in him. He hated the thought of ascending the mountain, but his need for food quashed any ideas he had about figuring a way down. He stepped back from the cliff and headed back up the mountain.

At the bottom of the first switchback, Peter spat out the remains of his cud of coca and looked at the sun arcing down the western sky. He raised his fingers toward the sun and attempted to tell the time, but again the quick calculation was not there. His best estimate was around two in the afternoon. It was not exact but was probably within twenty minutes either way—close enough. That gave him somewhere around five hours of daylight. Five hours to find Tian's hut, and if he was lucky, find him there. Or maybe he would run into Yachay.

But his gut told him he was on his own from here on, that he had used up his luck on the way up, and it was he and this mountain with his life in the balance.

He removed his backpack. He would rest for a just a moment. Fatigue gnawed at his shoulders and down his arms and legs like an insidious disease. This was different from before. Then he had been plenty tired, near exhaustion at one point, but he had Aldo with him and destiny or luck or, as Pavor would have him believe, Viracocha looking after him.

Whatever it was, it had departed and left him alone. He needed to collect himself, to calm himself, for fear was contributing to his fatigue. Aldo had provided an inner confidence that no longer accompanied Peter, and he must fight the fear.

Peter stood as a shiver ran through him. The temperature was much colder than at the bridge, and the ever-changing sky had the look of snow. He removed his windbreaker from the backpack and put it on. As much as he fought the thought, he missed the comfort of the red poncho, which had felt like a security blanket.

He strapped on his backpack and started back up the first switchback. He tried to stay focused on getting to Tian's place. *Don't think. Just walk,* he told himself as he took on the first zigzag up the mountain.

He stayed close to the mountain side of the trail, walking into chaotic gusts of swirling wind that funneled up loose snow before fading away. One after another, like snow devils they danced around Peter as he came to a halt to cover his face. A few steps forward, stop and catch his breath, a few steps forward ...

After an hour of this, he found refuge in a recess in the side of the mountain that provided shelter from the cold, bitter wind. He thought about going back down where he might find warmer air and better conditions. A nervous edge of hunger in his stomach weighed on his decision—food above, none below. Could he find his way down, all the way down, without food? As he weighed his options, the wind died down.

He stepped out of the little alcove into calm air. There wasn't a trace of the swirling snow. He headed back up the mountain.

By the time he completed the first switchback, it had started to snow. The valley was not visible, covered in a blanket of mist. Never had he felt so isolated and far from home. He wished he had looked for a way down the mountain from the bridge, to get closer to his escape instead of walking back into the maw of this mountainous beast.

Stay steady. Stay strong, he told himself. He could not afford to second-guess himself at this stage, for there was no turning back.

His best estimation was that he had three, maybe three and a half, hours of daylight left. And that was only a guess, for the sun was nowhere to be seen, as the sky was shrouded in gray.

One thing he didn't have to guess was that he needed to pick up the pace, low energy or not. And though he had not eaten since morning and was tired, sore, and fighting his nerves, he must endure.

The footing on the second switchback was reasonable, and his boots provided good traction. But the snowfall was picking up, and visibility was only a couple of feet. He blocked out everything around him and concentrated on the trail ahead and striding hard, one step and then the next ...

He lost himself in the rhythm of the task at hand. He didn't snap out of it until he stopped at the end of the second switchback.

Whew, was he tired and hungry—very hungry. What he would not give for cold potatoes and quinoa. He checked his coca bag on his hip. Better save it for the days ahead, in case he was really in a desperate situation. "Hah." Peter laughed aloud at the thought of it getting any more desperate. He was in the middle of a storm that threatened a blizzard, he had no food, the temperature was dropping, and still there was a ways to go to Tian's hut.

The sky had cleared enough to see the outline of mountains in the distance, and of course the incessant snow was beginning to blow sideways from wind gusts. But the sun and the land below were hidden from view.

It was getting personal: Peter Richards versus the mountain. It angered him that this was happening, the forces of nature lined up against him. "Son of a bitch," he said under his breath.

If this mountain intended to take him out, he would make it earn its victory. He pulled his backpack up higher on his shoulders, took a deep breath, and began walking higher up this damn mountain.

The wind picked up and started swirling those infernal whirlwinds that seemed to dance around him, spitting out icy granules in his face. He kept his head down, one step and then another, one step and then another …

By dusk, his movements grew slow and exaggerated. Everything took longer, even his thought processes. He was somewhere in the middle of the third switchback, or was it the fourth? My God, he was not sure.

He stopped for a moment and thought back. He remembered completing the first and not being able to see the valley below. At the end of the second, the sky had cleared enough so that the mountains in the distance were visible. Did he finish the third and forget? No, he must still be on the third. There was no way he could make it to Tian's.

His challenge to the mountain had relaxed his body and mind and gotten him to this point. But now his weakened muscles screamed for him to stop, especially his knees. His stomach felt queasy, and his appetite was gone. And his hands were starting to feel numb, he could hardly feel his feet, and his face felt like a block of ice. He touched it and wiped away bits of perspiration and snow that had frozen into tiny bits of ice. He was so intent he hadn't even noticed them.

He began to shiver, and goose bumps tingled his arms. He had to start moving soon. The question was where. It soon would be night, and the temperature would plummet even more.

He had to find shelter, for he would not be able to find his way to Tian's hut at night.

A strong wind blew directly at him as if the mountains were blowing breaths of cold air. He was so tired he was having trouble focusing. He needed to find a cave or some opening in the mountain to offer him shelter from the cold.

He was on a level section and started walking, scanning up the mountainside looking for any sort of opening. His movements were slowing down, as he couldn't get his body to go any faster than one step, stop, one step, stop. Then he remembered somewhere down the trail, he had spotted a cave-like opening fifteen or twenty feet overhead.

He started back for it, not exactly sure how long ago he had passed it. A pang of dark humor whisked through him at the fact that he was descending the mountain for the second time this day.

He kept one eye on the trail and the other up the mountainside for the cave as he took a step, looked, took a step, looked.

He stumbled twice in his search, once almost falling. His shivering made it difficult to concentrate, and he had to remind himself what he was looking for and where exactly he was. At last he saw it, a cave-like opening overhead, well out of his reach. The wall had a five-foot-high ledge abutting a sheer of rock fifteen feet high. Crevices and juts of rocks along the wall would provide good gripping points and footholds.

He searched for a path with crevices and footholds along the way. If he scaled up to the left, then right, and back to the left, he would be right below the hole. *Left, right, left,* he told himself.

He was so damn cold, his arm and leg joints were stiffening, and the light was fading fast. Time was of the essence. He took a moment to gain some strength and to concentrate. Climb up and get into that hole.

He dropped his backpack, lowered his chest on the ledge, and shimmied himself up. He took a moment to catch his breath. He leaned his body flat against the wall of rock, reached up to his left, and got his fingers into a crevice. He lifted his boot into a crevice and pulled himself up with every ounce of strength he could muster. He gasped for air, his chest pounding against the rock as if his heart would erupt.

When his breathing slowed, he reached to his right for another crevice but brought his arm down, as he needed more time to gather strength. He waited for a moment and then reached up and put his fingers in the opening, but he couldn't feel them in it. *Get yourself up into that hole.*

He pulled himself up, his foot resting on a knob of jutting rock. So far, so good. One more and he would make it. He leaned his head back to find another crevice and looked to his left, or was it right? "Left, right, left," he said under his breath. There, overhead to his left at a forty-five-degree angle was an opening to place his fingers and an inviting little shelf of rock below it for his foot.

He reached out his left arm, stretching for the opening but not quite there. He stood on his toes, stretching and leaning, when his feet slipped. Instinctively, he pushed away from the mountainside with his hands, crashing onto the bottom ledge on his side, and tumbling onto the trail, landing awkwardly on his left ankle. A bolt of pain shot up his leg. He nearly blacked out.

The pain subsided to a dull throb in his ankle. Peter sat up and caught his breath. His shoulder and side were sore but seemed okay, as were his upper body and arms. He pulled up the bottom of his pants and touched his ankle. It was already starting to swell and painful to touch. He didn't think it was broken, but he realized a bad sprain was nothing to sneer at. He got to one knee, put his weight on his good foot, and stood. He took a step, gingerly extending the foot with the damaged ankle, and again the shooting pain ran up his leg.

Okay, he needed not to panic and to figure something out. This wasn't insurmountable. He remembered a recess back down a ways. Yes, he would have to crawl a bit, but once he got away from the wind ... *and what's this, hail?* A flurry of BB-sized ice pellets blew sideways in the wind. Peter got down on his hands and knees and started crawling back down the trail.

The ankle throbbed so bad that he got down on his chest and crawled with his arms pulling him forward. One arm forward and then repeat. One arm forward and then repeat. He continued like this into the night. By the time he reached where he thought the recess was, he couldn't find it. He could no longer feel the bits of hail riddling his face. He had to find that recess. Peter struggled up into a sitting position. The moon had peeked out and provided just enough light to scan around and try to get his bearings.

He remembered now that he had seen the recess near a boulder that jutted onto the trail. Didn't he pass a boulder crawling down the mountain? Could he have possibly passed the opening and not seen it? He had been so intent on one arm then another that he hadn't been paying close attention.

He looked back up the trail, and there was a boulder jutting out. He got back on his belly and started again. One hand forward and then pull with the other. It was so damn tiring dragging himself up.

Finally he came to the boulder and didn't see a recess anywhere—nothing but a sheer wall of rock. He crawled farther, and still there was none.

He would rest for a minute. He rolled on his side and sat up with his back against a sheer of rock. The hail and snow had stopped. The incessant wind remained, but the fog and mist had gone, and the moon shined over the valley, a neutral gray stretch of land with intersecting streaks of long black shadows. In the distance, the tips of mountains shone blue in the moonlight.

He was breathing heavily, almost gasping for air. My God, he was tired, so damn tired. Where had he left his backpack? He couldn't remember if it was up or down the mountain.

Finally, his breathing slowed, but he was feeling a tingling numbness in his extremities. His vision blurred, he wiped a crusty layer of ice off his brow. Everywhere he looked, mountains. He checked his bad ankle and couldn't feel his own touch on it. He reached over and put both hands around it—it was the size of a softball.

Okay, he would head down the mountain. No more going up. But first, he would rest for a few moments and let his mind settle.

What a strange and wonderful and bittersweet journey it had all been indeed. Peter closed his eyes for just a bit to relax and breathe easy and then to figure—yes, to figure—his way out of this. The wind blew loose snow into his face, but no longer could he feel it clinging. No longer did he feel the bitter wind or the biting cold invade his body. Oh, how sleep called to him.

Tomorrow he would wake refreshed, his ankle better, and he would begin walking again. He would find his way to the mountain base and Aldo's car. Could he drive with this bad ankle? He laughed aloud. Get there first, and then worry about driving to Lima and then to the airport.

He couldn't wait to get home to tell Bob Goodman over beers and horseshoes about this adventure. *Bob, you wouldn't believe the things I saw, the things I felt. It was a great journey.* And to stargaze with Devon and to hold Debra's hand and tell her how much, how damn much, he loved that good woman. Peter searched the sky, and there they were—the Pleiades. How appropriate.

A strong and unyielding sense came over Peter that Devon was stargazing at this very moment in the backyard with his classmates. God, how he wanted to be there, but there would be many more opportunities to stand on the platform shoulder to shoulder with his beloved boy. And to wrap his arms around Debra, to feel her touch and be in her company again.

In his search for a miracle, Peter had discovered a part of himself that he never knew existed—that different current of life from which he had drawn a heightened sensitivity and vitality, a sense of eternal reassurance that he had lived a past life as Padura. He was no longer one man in one closed world, but was fate so cruel as to abandon him on the side of a mountain after all that he had learned on his journey? There was so much to ponder, but for just a moment he would listen to the mountain whisper its secrets in his ear. For in the silence of the mountain there is much you can learn.